The Duke clut[...] closer in his a[...] head to kiss tha[...]

Leslie, who had by now forgotten her own name, accepted and returned the kiss with fevered delight, then leaned back against the firm grip which was binding her.

The move had an interesting effect. Hard lips came down again against her own, crushing, demanding. When they finally released her mouth, Leslie was almost without thought. Dimly she heard her own voice asking, "What is that scent you are using, Drogo? It is . . . quite intoxicating."

"Are you saying I make you drunk?"

"I am saying," stammered the bewildered girl, "that you had better release me before I do something . . . silly."

Fawcett Crest Books
by Elizabeth Chater:

THE DUKE'S DILEMMA

Elizabeth Chater

FAWCETT CREST • NEW YORK

A Fawcett Crest Book
Published by Ballantine Books
Copyright © 1986 by Elizabeth Chater

Library of Congress Catalog Card Number: 86-91183

ISBN: 0-449-20749-8

Manufactured in the United States of America

First Edition: November 1986

Chapter 1

Lawyer Muir looked up expectantly as the door to his inner sanctum swung open sharply, and a magnificent male figure strode arrogantly into the musty room.

That the visitor was angry was immediately apparent. Samuel Muir thought he had seldom seen such blazing eyes in a human face—pure golden fire! And as the big, tawny-haired fellow stalked across the floor and seated himself without an invitation on a chair facing the desk, Muir experienced a slight frisson of alarm even while he reminded himself that his behavior had been faultlessly professional.

An uncomfortable silence stretched between the two men.

Finally Drogo Trevelyan said coldly, "You sent for me, Muir? I was under the impression we had settled all my late parents' business six months ago." The voice and the expression on the man's countenance were under careful control, but the slight narrowing of heavy lids over the blazing eyes indicated anger close to the surface.

Summoning up his courage, Lawyer Muir said quietly, "I thank you for answering my request for a meeting so promptly, Your Grace. I hope you will accept my word that I would not have asked you to come here today had I not received some . . . rather disturbing information."

"Not some further evidence of my unlamented father's idiocy, I hope?" Trevelyan said nastily. "I had hoped we had settled all that! I told you I should not care to reopen Kenelm Place. It may fall to rack and ruin with my heartiest approval—"

1

"Someone is trying to buy it," interrupted Muir. "Much of the common land around the estate has already been sold. One or two of the smaller domains in the county, which border upon your holdings, have a new owner. And last week I received an offer for Kenelm."

"From whom?" demanded the duke sharply. "Why have I not been advised of this . . . activity?"

The lawyer forbore to remind his irascible client that the latter had given express instructions that he was not to be bothered with any further details about the estate. Instead he addressed himself to the first question.

"Possibly the most puzzling aspect of the situation," admitted the lawyer, "is the fact that we cannot discover who the purchaser of all these properties is. He is represented by an extremely . . . *astute*"—his tone expressed strong disapproval—"member of my profession, who is unwilling to divulge the name of his client. I would have asked you to discuss this matter with me sooner, milord, but I had hoped to have more specific information for you. As it is, my clerks have discovered that the . . . ah . . . purchaser has secured several parcels of land, enough to completely surround Your Grace's estate, with one exception."

The blond giant seated across the desk relaxed for the first time since he had entered the lawyer's chambers. Settling his big frame more comfortably in the armchair, he stared at his man-of-law. It was plain that the little mystery of the Unknown Purchaser had been enough to banish the anger the duke had felt at being summoned by Muir. A light of interest glowed in the striking eyes, and the handsome face relaxed into a faint grin.

"Are you suggesting that the mysterious owner of the one unsold piece of property may be trying to control the whole county, Muir? Which estate is it, by the way?"

"It is the ancestral estate of the Earls of Endale, Your Grace," replied Muir. "You may not have heard—traveling abroad for the last few years as you have been—that the former holder of the title was killed in a very unusual accident just a few months ago. The current earl is a boy of nine. His guardian is, I believe, a distant relative, and next in line for the title."

There was a short silence as the two men considered the situation.

Then the duke said, slowly, "I had made a decision never to return to a place which held nothing but ugly memories for me—as you are no doubt aware, Muir."

The lawyer raised his shaggy gray eyebrows. "I have indeed been made aware of Your Grace's decision." He nodded grimly. "Still, in this rather unusual set of circumstances, perhaps—?" He peered at his client from under his eyebrows.

His Grace the Duke of Kenelm rose to his full noble height and stretched as un-selfconsciously as a great cat. A rather savage grin twisted his well-shaped lips. "You have managed to arouse my interest, Muir! I think I shall travel down into the wilds of Sussex and investigate this mystery of the Unknown Purchaser. If I dislike him sufficiently, I may even permit him to buy Kenelm Place. That will teach him to covet other men's property! You may instruct your clerks to prepare a full report of whatever information you have been able to collect, and bring it to my town house tomorrow morning." With a casual nod of the leonine head, the duke departed, leaving his man-of-law to stare at the empty doorway with a curiously satisfied smirk.

Chapter 2

The Earl of Endale was crying.

As a general rule, he was well able to control his emotions, and had indeed been demonstrating that control surprisingly well during the last forty-eight hours of desperate flight, but even a self-possessed nine-year-old may be forgiven for breaking down a little when he is hungry, bitterly cold and wet, and badly frightened because his eldest sister lies unconscious at his feet.

Lord Daryl, the Right Honorable the Earl of Endale, knelt down and pulled her head up against his shoulder. "Leslie!" he cried. "Wake up! Are you sick? Oh, *Leslie!*"

From behind him, inside the great hole in the blasted oak tree, where Leslie had just finished tucking his other two sisters on beds of hastily gathered leaves, came the faintest of whimpers. It was enough to remind him of his role as Protector and Head of the Family.

"Don't *you* start crying," he commanded his fourteen-year-old sister Hilary, who was notoriously prone to emotional excesses. Daryl was well aware that he had better take firm charge of the situation or have a chorus of wailing sisters joining his own cry of dismay. He tried for the light touch, which Leslie had so carefully drilled in him all his life. He drew a steadying breath and spoke quietly.

"It is bad enough for *me* to be a watering pot, Hilary, without you and Meredith adding to the damp!"

A hesitant chuckle from Hilary greeted his feeble sally. Then Meredith, the sensible ten-year-old, rallied to his assistance. She said practically, "That branch must have struck her when she was trying to drag it down to hide our refuge. Let's pull her inside the shelter and try to keep warm by huddling together. Could we make a fire, Daryl, do you think?"

"I doubt we could get one started in this cloudburst," the earl answered, beginning at once to haul his sister's limp form into the gaping hole in the tree trunk. Meredith assisted him neatly, going first and cradling Leslie's head with loving care. She even darted outside once more and dragged the heavy, rotting tree limb against the opening of the shelter.

"Now *no one* will be able to tell that we have taken refuge in here." She nodded her satisfaction.

"Do you . . . suppose Leslie will . . . wake up soon?" quavered Hilary. "Oh, what shall we do if she . . . if she . . ."

At this very crucial moment, Leslie stirred and uttered a faint moan of pain. All three of her siblings gathered close to her in the dim light, patting or stroking any portion of her they could reach, and murmuring reassurances. Leslie opened her eyes, blinked rapidly to clear her vision, and peered at her companions. A lovely smile warmed and transformed her pale face.

"We are safe!" she breathed. She bent a particularly admiring smile upon the earl, ignoring the tearstains on his cheeks. "Thank you, Endale! I knew you could manage the thing!"

The earl blushed, but refused to accept the praise. "It was Meredith and Hilary who helped drag you inside. They were brave and quick."

"You are all heroes—or heroines, as the case may be." The seventeen-year-old girl managed a weak chuckle. Her head was still ringing oddly from the blow of the heavy branch, but she realized how important a calm demeanor was at this moment. "Now we must share some food and then try to snuggle together for warmth, dear ones. It will soon be dawn, I think, and we are safely hidden in this cozy refuge! Perhaps we can even fall asleep for a few hours.''

Pulling open the heavy bag that she had tied around her slender waist, Leslie portioned out the last of the oaten cakes she had snatched from the manor kitchen two nights ago, just before she led her brother and sisters away from the home that had become a terrifying prison to them all. The children were now so hungry and tired that they munched the food without stopping to talk. When every last crumb had been devoured, Leslie brought out the earthenware flagon she had taken, and carefully removed the stopper.

"What Miss Wheaton would say to my giving you French brandy, I can imagine only too well!'' she teased, as she offered a tiny sip to each child. "However, it is *warming*, and will help us all to get some sleep.'' She drained the last small portion herself.

Then, gathering the children to her with loving arms, she instructed them all to sleep quietly, for they must be as silent and wary as baby birds in a nest.

Whether because of the brandy, the exhaustion of their little bodies, or the warmth of Leslie's love, within a few minutes the children were fast asleep, huddling close to the big sister who had stolen them out of the dangerous situation in which they had found themselves.

Although she was wearier than she had ever been in her life, Leslie found that she could not close her eyes. Images of the last terrible weeks kept rising in her memory. As though the unexpected, terrible death of their beloved parents had not been agony enough, the resultant new regime, under the guardianship of their father's cousin, March Wardell, ushered in a time of such fear and insecurity as the young Endales had never experienced. The Wardells had appeared on the very day after the fatal accident, and announced to the stunned servants that they would be taking over the manor and the children. They refused to let the children attend the funeral, explaining that they were too young to be subjected to such a painful situation. When the family lawyer arrived to read the will, March Wardell sat in the library beside the nine-year-old inheritor of the title, and suggested reasonably enough that he, as the next in line, had better take up residence and manage affairs until the boy reached his majority. *Twelve years!*

Leslie shivered now, in the hollow of the tree, as she had done then, seated properly behind the new earl and his cousin March Wardell. How could any of them bear the domination of this frightening man for twelve years? Yet what could she say? The lawyer was explaining to them all that since the former earl, thinking himself too young to worry about such matters, had appointed no official guardian, it might be expedient to accept the kindly offer of the next of kin. The lawyer, although he had not previously met Mr. Wardell, had done some inquiring into his bona fides before coming down to Endale from London. He had discovered, first, that Wardell was indeed the earl's cousin several degrees removed; second, that there was no scandal connected with his name in London, where he had been living for a number of years; and third, that he had two years previously married the daughter of a very prosperous merchant, recently deceased. In fact, both Wardells were still properly and appropriately robed in black.

The fact that there had been no commerce between the families did not remove the validity of the blood tie. With a well-concealed reluctance, Lawyer Nord informed the children that they were now to accept Mr. Wardell as their guardian, and render courteous obedience to him and to his wife, a silent female whose small black eyes were always decorously lowered.

For a while, absorbed as she had been in her grief for their parents, Leslie had not realized how thoroughly the new guardians were entrenching themselves. Old, faithful servants were dismissed, usually with a large gratuity, which caused the neighbors and the other servants to comment on the generosity of the *new man*. When Leslie began to be aware of what was going on, she did not at first feel apprehension, but rather, a sense of loss. But then she realized that it was the older servants, loyal and partisan,

7

who were being shipped to other parts of England, or settled into almshouses in more comfortable climes. And there began to grow in the girl a strong feeling that all was not the charity and light the Wardells were so busily proclaiming.

Her suspicions were aroused by the gradual hardening of their guardian's attitude toward the little earl. The boy was constantly being challenged, probed, tested—and harassed. Several times Leslie found him in his room, trying to stifle his tears in the heavy bolster on the great bed his parents had once shared. By dint of careful questioning, she got him to admit that Cousin Wardell was constantly reminding him that his father was dead, and that the son was not a fit replacement, either in talent, temperament, or age.

After one of these sessions, when she had left the exhausted little boy asleep, Leslie realized that she would have to heed the increasing number of signs that all was not well. She did not, at that point, entertain the fears she was soon to develop. It was after March brought home the new stallion he had bought for the earl, and with it a heavy-featured groom, that all her doubts and fears were resolved into a desperate determination.

Of course, all the family came out to the stables to see the gift. Mrs. Wardell, as usual silent, but with a meek, nervous smile on her lips, had bought a new riding habit for her husband's ward. When she had him dressed in it, she led him out to the stables, where March waited to throw the boy up on his new horse. Daryl was a brave boy, but Leslie felt a real chill of alarm as she saw how very small he looked upon the big animal. March presented him with a new, silver-topped whip. Then, with a wide, mirthless smile, he shouted, *"Go, Endale!"* and struck the stallion with his own crop.

Leslie did not hear her own cry as she raced out of the stables after the galloping horse. The beast was pounding across the rough cobbles of the stableyard, sparks flying as his great, metal-shod hooves struck the stones. He was headed directly for the stone wall.

Frozen with horror, she knew the child would not be able to handle the terrified animal, yet she was powerless to aid Daryl or to turn away from the sight of his small body as he sawed away on the reins and called out to the beast.

And then, beast and boy, they were over the wall.

A few heartbeats later, the horse came into view, riderless, careening across the inner paddock.

Leslie's eyes went to the face of their guardian. There was nothing to be read from his expression, neither proper anxiety nor sly gratification. It was such a blank, shuttered countenance as Leslie had never seen. And then his eyes met hers, and he was wearing the self-possessed smile with which they were all familiar. Calling the horrified grooms and stableboys to follow, he led the way at a run toward the wall.

Leslie was at his shoulder all the way.

When they reached the wall, it was to see a small, crumpled form in the bushes that grew wild against the far side. While Leslie was scrambling over, her brother lifted his small head and stared, dazed, up into her face.

"I fell," he said slowly. "I lost the reins."

"I've never seen a neater toss," Leslie said cheerfully, before anyone else could speak. "Let me check you for bruises now, Endale, and then we'll have you back up again before that *untamed beast* has time to decide he has bested you!" Her eyes moved quickly around the circle of faces bending above the earl. *On every face, even March's, was surprise and a dawning respect.* Leslie kept her glance on March for a moment, trying to catch and hold his eyes, but his glance slid beyond her and fastened on the boy.

"Are you sure you are not hurt?" There was no note of warmth in the flat voice. "Perhaps you should let me carry you back to the house."

"Thank you, sir, I am well enough." Daryl managed a smile as he pulled himself to his feet. "Endale doesn't give up that easily, you know!" he added, and was rewarded by a spontaneous cheer from the assembled servants.

"No," said Wardell, and he carried the boy to his room.

After that day, Leslie knew she must get Daryl away as quickly as possible. Yet now, wet, cold, hungry, she wondered if her wild plan would result in even greater harm for the earl.

She did not close her eyes until long after dawn broke, gray with swollen clouds and occasional heavy showers.

Chapter 3

Drogo Trevelyan moved restlessly against the squabs of his elegant carriage as it jolted and lurched its way into the country. Night was falling, and a cold, miserable, rainy night it was promising to be. He had been delayed in leaving London, having found the report brought to his town house by Samuel Muir's clerk to be as provocative as the lawyer had indicated. He took time to read it carefully, and spent another hour deciding upon his own course of action.

There was another reason for his delay, which the young Duke refused to acknowledge—a powerful reluctance to return to his ancestral home.

Drogo and his father had never seen eye to eye about anything during the whole of their stormy relationship. The old duke, a late convert to a covenanting sect after a rake-helly youth and a dissolute middle age, had raged self-righteously every time a new rumor concerning his only son's profligacy reached him—which was every time the post was delivered or an acquaintance called. Members of the ton, many of whom had suffered the caustic tongue or the cruel behavior of the former roué, enjoyed taunting him with *on dits* about the flagrant exploits of his heir. *Like father, like son,* they would snicker or sneer.

At first Drogo, unable to believe in the pious diatribes to which he was subjected every time he encountered his papa, tried to avoid such encounters by staying away from Kenelm Place as much as possible. The crisis came when Drogo attempted to run a rig against his best friend, Lord

Philip Sandron, at a hunt dinner and ball attended by a galaxy of social stars. True, Drogo was bored, and jealous of his friend's good fortune in securing as his wife a darling girl whom Drogo had hoped to make his own mistress. It was a nasty little trick he had attempted to play, but unfortunately for him, his plan failed—publicly.

Of course, half the guests at the ball had rushed to report the embarrassing incident to the old duke. He had summoned his son to Kenelm Place and issued an ultimatum. Any further licentious behavior would result in the immediate stoppage of the heir's allowance, and confinement to his father's estate until further notice.

Sore from the public humiliation, and suffering, oddly enough, pangs of conscience that he refused to admit, Drogo left for the Continent that very day, without bidding anyone farewell or even announcing his departure to his father. Luckily for the angry young man, he had ample funds from his mother's estate to cushion him for the rest of his life, if need be.

In the event, he only needed them for three years, during which time he made a name for himself in the more sophisticated capitals of Europe. One morning, awaking late with a wretched head from his indulgences of the night before, he was handed a message from his family's man-of-law to the effect that, his father being deceased, Drogo was the new Duke of Kenelm, and his presence in London was most urgently required.

He had come back to England, and those who remembered his earlier excesses were agog to watch what they hoped would be even more outrageous behavior. In this they were, surprisingly, disappointed. Oh, Drogo Trevelyan was even better looking than he had been three years earlier, big and tawny-blond and powerful, but the roguish gleam was gone from his golden eyes, the ready smile from his well-cut lips, and he no longer took his pleasures flamboyantly. He had acquired, either by painful experience or deliberate design, a cool, daunting, cynical facade, which effectively concealed his emotions.

Even in the darkening shadows of his elegant coach, the

12

young duke's handsome face revealed nothing of the distaste he felt at the very thought of reentering a house that had never been a home to him. His mother, an Austrian aristocrat, had become in her later years a chronic invalid, more distressed by the wretched climate and hopelessly dull society of England than by her husband's notorious infidelities. His father, when he deigned to notice his family, was selfish, cruel, and insensitive. In fact, for Drogo, Kenelm Place was the scene of the most unhappy experiences of his life. It had been almost with relief that he had heard his father's ultimatum. On that day, Drogo had resolved never to return to his father's home again.

Yet here he was, going back to the decaying monument to Trevelyan arrogance. Well, he wouldn't be expected to stay there, thank God! The very thought of the leaking roof, the cobwebbed rooms, the dusty, sour-smelling furniture, caused Drogo to wrinkle his fine, straight nose in disgust. He had sent a groom riding ahead to book a suite of rooms at the Kenelm Arms, the best inn the county boasted. Tonight he would dine well, and drink enough of the run-brandy to insure a sound sleep. Tomorrow would be soon enough to call upon the neighborhood intelligencers and listen to gossip about the mysterious stranger who was buying up property. It might even be that he would not have to go near Kenelm Place at all.

Chapter 4

Leslie permitted herself to doze only briefly during the long day, rousing herself frequently to observe the condition of the children. Their little faces, pale and strained even in slumber, tore at her heart. Had she made a dreadful mistake in removing them clandestinely from their home? Were her suspicions of their guardian only silly nonsense, built out of loneliness and loss and adolescent fears? What if her action in stealing her brother and sisters from the only home they had ever known should result in illness or injury?

Then her natural strength of character would rouse itself, and she would remind herself that anything, even such rough usage as they were facing, was better than one more day's stay in a house that had been subtly taken over by the blandly smiling March Wardell and his silent wife. Remembering March's fixed smirk and hooded eyes, Leslie knew that no precautions could be too great to protect her brother and sisters from that mockery of concern.

She had no need to remind herself that the cousin-guardian was the *next heir to the earldom after Daryl.*

Why had she not found the courage to mention her fears to any of her parents' friends? Leslie sighed. *No one would have believed her, and she knew it.* She had to admit that Cousin March had not made a single overtly hostile move against his ward. he had lost no time in presenting himself to the neighborhood as a kind and considerate man. His servants made sure everyone heard of the gift of a fine new horse to console the newly orphaned earl. It was surely not Wardell's fault that the horse had turned out to be a vicious brute, or that Daryl's inevitable fall might have caused the boy serious injury or death. After all, the guardian had refused permission for the boy to try to remount the savage animal—as his oldest sister so irresponsibly had urged— lest further injury might occur. The demeaning effect of that refusal on the boy was not mentioned.

Nor could blame be put upon the alarmed guardian when a fire broke out in Daryl's bedroom the very night after the incident with the horse. The blaze might have had serious consequences had not Leslie, sleeping in the room next to Daryl's, noticed the smoke and dashed in to rescue her little brother. The next morning Wardell invited several of their neighbors to share coffee and honor the heroine of the event. He spoke gently of an excited child's nightmare, and an overturned candle. Or—with a forgiving smile—of a child's natural love of mischief, perhaps? After all, the boy had been unhappy at his guardian's refusal to let him remount the gift-horse. There was a general shaking of heads, and one or two rather minatory glances at the young earl, brought in to assure family friends that he was indeed safe. When someone asked if the cause of the fire had been determined, March said regretfully that the bedroom had been almost completely gutted before the sleepy servants could be organized to put the fire out.

The County bigwigs, who had been inclined to resent the arrival of March Wardell and his plebeian wife into their closed little society, began to say that the heir was showing a good deal of patience with his young charges, considering their behavior. Leslie was not sure how the rumors had started, but one of her mother's old friends paid her a visit especially to advise her to restrain her brother's resentment, and that of her sisters, against their guardian.

"For you must admit, Leslie, that the poor man was not to blame for your papa's accident, and he and that wife of his are trying to protect and advise you to the best of their ability," Lady Dilvish admonished her. "It cannot be an

15

easy thing to be saddled with the responsibility and care of four children, when one has never had any of one's own!''

Leslie agreed quietly that it must indeed be a burden, and that she would make sure her siblings were reminded of their manners. But even as she spoke, the girl felt a dreadful conviction that the fall from the horse and the unexplained fire had not been accidents at all, but cold-blooded attacks upon her brother's life.

And so she had concocted the plan to escape from their breached and endangered home, and to hide out in the now deserted mansion of the Duke of Kenelm. Its former master, a wicked man well hated in the county in which he had been the most powerful nobleman, had died a few months ago. It was public knowledge that the old reprobate had joined an obscure religious cult in his latter days, and had been, moreover, as mad as a March hare for years.

His son, banished by the father three years earlier for reasons Leslie could only speculate upon, had never come back, even for his father's funeral. County gossip said he had vowed never to return, but to let his ancestral home fall into decay. True enough, the place was in a wretched state of disrepair. The only custodian was a surly middle-aged fellow named Dawls, who had been hired by Lawyer Muir to keep a token watch over the estate. Dawls lived in the crumbling gate house near the front gateway and, according to village opinion, maintained a very casual surveillance indeed. Everyone said smugly that the estate was a disgrace to the neighborhood, and it was all the new duke's fault.

Leslie's plan, simply, had been to seek refuge for her siblings in the abandoned main residence, where surely March Wardell would never think of looking for them. She hoped to stay hidden there until it was safe to board a stagecoach for London, where her father's great-aunt, Lady Bella Endale, lived. This aged but socially impeccable female was the leader of a small, select coterie of dames who did not trouble their heads about the rest of the beau monde, since they knew themselves to be superior to all of it. The ancient female wielded a great deal of power. The fact that she had heartily disapproved of her great-nephew and his wife—she had not even deigned to attend their funeral—was not important, Leslie told herself. When the old woman was presented with the story of the vicious gift-horse and the mysterious fire in the young earl's bedroom, she would surely offer to house the children, her own flesh and blood, until a real investigation could be made. Certainly it would be impossible for Wardell to arrange an *accident* to the little earl while the boy was living in the old dragon's residence.

Pulling herself back to the grim present, Leslie was encouraged to observe that the children were sleeping more peacefully in their unconventional nest. They would be better able to bear the rigors of the coming night—the final one upon the road, Leslie hoped—after this short rest. The girl breathed a silent prayer for their safety until she could get them on a stagecoach for London.

Of course she would not try to wheedle sanctuary from Dawls. The man was reported to be a surly recluse, scarcely sparing a word to the tradespeople who sold him supplies. Had not Lawyer Muir continued to pay the bills without question, it is doubtful if any tradesman worthy of his salt would have given Dawls so much as the time of day. These facts being well-known, Leslie did not hope to enlist the active aid of the custodian. In fact, she had planned to sneak into the mansion before dawn. She had never visited Kenelm Place, but she'd heard enough, during her seventeen years at Endale, to have a pretty good idea of the architecture of the mansion, as well as its current state of disrepair.

Her plan was a simple one. As soon as it became dark enough, she would rouse her little band and set out for Kenelm Place. She expected to reach it before dawn. Once within the building, she would make her sisters and brother comfortable in the cleanest of the bedrooms. No matter how dusty the furniture, the beds would at least be softer and drier than wet leaves and damp moss! Then, while the children rested, Leslie would find water for them to drink and wash in when they awoke, and food they could eat.

17

There must be pantries and storerooms that would still hold remnants of the providence of the former housekeeper; if not, there were root cellars or even the neglected home farm to be searched for enough food to sustain life until the little party reached London.

Once she had them in the stagecoach, Leslie was sure she could manage. Pinned within her bodice she had a silk purse containing several coins, gifts from her father during happier times, surely more than enough for the fare. As for clean clothing to replace the wet, dirty garments they now wore—which would proclaim to all and sundry that they were waifs or even fugitives—Leslie had an idea she could find a supply. Had not Miss Wheaton, who had been their governess until Cousin Wardell dismissed her, once mentioned the treasures to be found in the extensive attics of all great houses? And had she not proved her point by leading the wide-eyed children up to the vast spaces beneath the roof of their own beloved home, and opening the trunks and boxes full of fascinating objects, costumes of velvet and silk, absurd shoes, carved ivory fans, reticules, even a carved wooden box containing two pistols? There were treasures enough to keep the young Endales entertained throughout one long rainy day.

Leslie assured herself that there would be similar trunks in the attics at Kenelm. She set her small jaw firmly as she considered that she would raid them ruthlessly for the benefit of the fugitives. No one cared what happened to the Place or anything in it, she reminded herself. Certainly not its legal owner, the licentious Duke of Kenelm, who had been widely quoted as saying that the whole house could fall to rack and ruin with his blessing!

But of course, he would never know that his little-regarded belongings were going to serve a useful purpose for some of the neighbors he so openly disdained.

Chapter 5

Everyone at the Kenelm Arms, from its host, George Cross, to the lowliest kitchen drudge, was aware of the exact moment when Drogo Trevelyan, the Most Noble the Duke of Kenelm, entered the premises. Had not His Grace's groom informed all and sundry that his master would be arriving shortly, and wouldn't relish being fobbed off with anything less than the best rooms in the house? This had been said with an overweening pomposity that set everyone's teeth on edge, and did absolutely nothing to redeem the unpleasant reputation that the county's most important nobleman already bore.

However, a duke was a duke, and his money was as good as anyone else's, and probably more plentiful than most. Host Cross came forward to bid his noble guest welcome, but found his fawning servilities halting on his lips as he absorbed the impact of the massive, handsome male striding toward him, the light from the inn lamps turning his unpowdered hair to shining gold. A closer look at the cat-yellow eyes trained so dauntingly upon his own countenance further disconcerted the innkeeper.

There was a brief, uncomfortable silence.

Then His Grace said quietly, "I am Kenelm. I presume my rooms are ready?"

Thus prodded, Host Cross turned without another word and led the way to the best suite of rooms the house boasted. From the silent scrutiny these received, the duke was not impressed.

"Will there be anything . . . Can I get Your Worship a bite to eat?" Cross faltered.

"Rather more than a bite, I should hope," said the duke coldly, in a tone that bore witness to the fact that he did not expect much from such a raggle-taggle establishment.

"Within ten minutes, Your Grace," promised Cross, anxious to remove himself from so much overpowering arrogance as quickly as possible. He exhaled heavily on his way down the stairs, and mopped his red face, but managed to present at least an appearance of savoir faire to the eagerly clustering servants and village loungers gathered in the great hallway and spilling in from the ordinary in hopes of some crumbs of information. He got a good deal of satisfaction out of dispersing these gape-seeds and, a trifle restored in self-esteem, bustled into the kitchen to demand the finest cuisine the cook could produce.

"And I only hope it's worth eating, Mrs. Cross," he warned his flustered wife. "That one's a Tartar, and no mistake! Worse than his pa ever was!"

The object of this commotion strode through the inn's finest suite with an air of scornful dissatisfaction, then turned to his silent valet with a terse command to get him out of his greatcoat and set up water for washing. By the time the first of the inn waiters made a timid knocking upon the door to the sitting room, the duke was more comfortably attired in well-fitting evening clothes. With the removal of his Hessian boots, His Grace's temper seemed to have improved a little, and he even gave the last and smallest of the maidservants a pleasant smile.

This had the effect of putting her into a delighted flutteration; she handed the hot loaf she carried directly to the duke, rather than to the senior waiter.

When the servants were finally sent from the room by the duke's valet, Parsons, Drogo lifted those tawny eyes from the feast that had been set up for him.

"Go down now and get your own meal," he advised Parsons. "And don't look so glum. The food's a damn sight better here than you'd get at Kenelm Place! If I had gone there, you would probably have found yourself doing the cooking and cleaning."

Drogo observed the look of horror on Parsons' face with the first grin that had crossed his lips in several days. After the valet left, however, the duke's countenance once more assumed its habitual arrogance. He bitterly resented having to return to the place that had never been home to him, which held no memories of joy or affection or even friendly companionship. Still, if someone was trying to steal out from under his nose the lands his family had owned for several hundred years, Drogo Trevelyan wished to know *who* was attempting the theft, and *why*.

Tomorrow he would visit the wretched pile. And then he would probably have to call upon some of the other landowners in the county, and try to find out what they knew of this Mysterious Purchaser. His well-cut lips curled disdainfully at the necessity of palavering with those rustic bumpkins, and he asked himself why he bothered to defend a holding that he had never loved nor wanted. Perhaps, he decided, it was because he had always been jealous of what was his own, and the idea of anyone daring to steal something that was his, even if he didn't want it himself, was enraging to him. The purchaser, whoever he was, had better have a good reason and offer a generous price. And even then, I shall probably refuse to sell, Drogo thought viciously. I would rather let the place fall into dust than see it belong to someone else.

Feeling not at all guilty over such a dog-in-the-manger-ish attitude, the duke finished his meal with an excellent smuggled brandy. He sat a long time over the cognac, his hooded golden eyes fixed blindly on the far wall, thinking about the few facts that Muir's clerks had been able to discover.

Chapter 6

The last hours of their secret flight were worse than anything that had gone before, Leslie thought, holding desperately to her self-control. The first disaster was missing the way through unfamiliar land, and losing two hours before she could reorient herself by the hazardous expedient of leaving the safe obscurity of the deep woods in order to find and follow one of the traveled roads.

To Leslie's alarm, when the little group did emerge cautiously near one of the country roads, they discovered it to be surprisingly busy. Granted, the rain had passed, and a full moon shone quite brightly in a cloud-free sky, making travel by coach or horseback quite possible. On the other hand, there was normally very little traffic upon these roads at night, as Leslie was well aware. She had carefully avoided the great highway to London, using only the less frequented lanes and byways when she was forced to leave the woods.

She had been so sure that March Wardell would not let the little earl slip out of his clutches without a struggle that she saw his stout, menacing shape in every shadow, and felt her nerves tingle at every sound she could not immediately identify. And now there were new challenges. The duke's estate was guarded by a high stone wall, so stoutly built that even years of neglect had not breached its security. It would be impossible for the children to climb it. There were two ways to get in, she knew: the massive front entrance, guarded by metal gates that had been, of late years, kept chained and locked; and the rear entrance, for servants, farmers, and tradespeople. These latter gates of stout wood were kept latched, true, but Leslie had heard mocking comments at the futility of such puny guards. What use to chain up the front like a fortress, sneered the villagers, when the rear gaped open night and day, an invitation to any Romany tinker who chanced to pass that way? Indeed, it was just such a derisory remark that had given the girl, desperate to protect her little brother, the idea for a possible refuge.

But tonight, in the revealing moonlight, it had not been easy to avoid the unusually heavy traffic upon the road that led around to the rear of the enormous estate. Alarmed by the increasing light that betokened the coming of dawn, and by the wordless exhaustion of her little group, Leslie decided to brave the easier going at the middle of the road.

She was leading her sisters and brother rapidly along when a muffled thudding of hooves caught her attention. The sounds came from behind her, and warned her that riders were approaching fast. Without a moment's hesitation, she gave the low command that she had taught the children meant instant obedience, and guided them off the road and into the underbrush. There was not even time for them to worm themselves into deeper hiding in the bushes before the thudding became the rapid pounding of horses' hooves.

More horses than one. Within moments, Leslie was privileged to behold her cousin March and Prenn, his groom, galloping toward her, faces grimly intent as they scanned the verges of the narrow road.

In a flashing moment the two riders were past and pounding away toward the rear of the estate. The girl caught her breath in a fearful gulp. She tried to compose herself as she faced the children huddling on the ground near her.

"I think we fooled them neatly," she heard herself saying, and marveled that her voice came out so firm and confident. "I'm proud of you! You would make good scouts for an army."

"I think *I* am going to be sick," announced Hilary in

23

anguished tones. "Did you see the way Cousin March was glaring at us? I was *sure* he had spotted us!"

"If he had, he would be here right now," countered Meredith reasonably. "Why would he ride on if he'd seen us?"

Hilary groaned at this sensible question, and refused to answer it. Instead she complained, "You are so *prosaic*, Meredith! Have you *no* sensitivity at all? Do you not realize that our very *lives* are in danger—?"

"That," said Leslie firmly, "will be quite enough of that, Hilary! We have diddled Cousin March very neatly. He and Prenn have gone; we are safe for the moment." She looked at Daryl, who was sitting silently under a bush, staring out at the road from a white, weary little face. As she watched him, he sneezed, violently, three times.

He is sick! her mind wailed. *I have made the boy ill with my insane scheme! I only wanted to protect him—*

Then common sense took over, and Leslie forced a smile. "Bless you, Daryl! I can see we must get under cover, all of us, if we wish to avoid putrid sore throats."

This threat, with its reminder of aching heads and bodies and painful coughing spells, brought all her little group to instant attention and willingness to obey. Leslie thought rapidly. Surely Cousin March could have no real knowledge of her goal, or indeed of her plan to escape. He must be totally confused, lashing about like an angry animal at their disappearance. Of course, the sudden absence of *all* the Endale children would be a nine days' wonder in the county, and even in London. Impossible to conceal such an event! The next heir would inevitably be questioned, challenged, whispered about. It was no wonder he was scouring the roads with that anxious glare! He *needed* to find them, and find them safe and sound, lest his own reputation be smirched. A fine guardian he was proving to be! Perhaps the coincidences of the savage horse and the destructive fire would assume a weightier significance when considered in conjunction with the total disappearance of the earl and his sisters.

Leslie took comfort in that thought. Still, she could not

rely upon aroused public curiosity to protect Daryl from his heir. It was most likely that March would furbish up some clever explanation for the loss of the children. A gypsy kidnapping, perhaps? Or worse, the willful flight of spoiled children too resentful of their kindly guardian to consider the pain and anxiety they were causing him! Leslie set her teeth. She would *never* permit them to be dragged back to Endale and held up to public censure as petulant ingrates! For one thing, the next contrived "accident" might prove fatal.

So. She could not take a chance on March finding them before they reached London and the safety of Lady Bella's residence. It was clear that March and his servants were out scouring the roads. No telling how many persons had been recruited to aid in the search, nor what plans the heir had. He could be simply covering all the roads, inquiring at every inn and hospital, even searching barns and out-buildings. Since he was on this road, used only as an access to the rear of Kenelm Place, might it be supposed that he suspected the children would try for sanctuary there? Leslie shook her head. She was convinced, perhaps by some desperation she had glimpsed in March's face as he flashed past, that her cousin was rushing about aimlessly, covering all the roads and byways in search of his quarry. Perhaps he even had his servants combing the woods and empty commons. They could be coming up behind her at this very moment!

Casting one worried glance to the rear, Leslie drew a sustaining breath. She must move forward quickly with her little party of refugees, and get them under cover. She turned to the silent, frightened children.

"This is not a setback," she told them quietly. "It seems to me that Cousin March is at his wit's end, and is riding the roads because he doesn't know what else to do. If he dares to invade the duke's estate, he will discover from Dawls that we have not been seen there—"

"And he'll be sent away with a flea in his ear," added Meredith with a grin. The surly custodian had earned a reputation in the neighborhood. "I wish I might be there to see it!"

Leslie smiled back at her sensible sister. "It's a great advantage to us if he's told we haven't been seen at Kenelm. That will turn Cousin March off, and leave us free to press on to our goal. Of course, we'll have to move through the bushes, and behind the hedgerows, instead of walking along the road—at least until we're sure Cousin March won't be back this way. . . ."

Daryl sneezed again, three deep, convulsive gasps that struck at Leslie's very heart. Taking his small, cold hand and Hilary's in her warmer ones, she smiled at Meredith and said brightly, "Tallyho! Endale is going to help his poor old sister through this murky dawn to safety!"

Wordlessly the little boy began to walk, eyes fixed grimly on the distant point where the rear entrance to the duke's estate broke the wall. It was, Leslie thought in despairing pity, the worst part of the whole nightmare attempt to escape. But if only they could reach the dilapidated Place, the worst would be over. She comforted herself with that hope as the dreadful journey dragged on.

In the event, Leslie's plan was accomplished with ridiculous ease. There was no one about when she laboriously unlatched the rear gates, swung them open, and led her brother and sisters inside the stableyard at Kenelm Place. Telling them to remain quiet until she made sure there would be no sign of their entry, she manhandled the massive, creaking gates closed again, and even succeeded in latching them. Then, after a swift reconnaissance, she led the subdued, exhausted children up to the kitchen entrance.

Again, anticlimax. The heavy door creaked open under her tentative pushing, and they slipped quietly into the shadowy great kitchen. Leslie swung the door shut and turned to grin joyously at the children.

"*Safe*, my dear ones! *We've done it!* Endale triumphant!'' she quoted the family motto. Weary little faces lit up in response to her smile of relief and satisfaction.

But Leslie did not relax her vigilance for a moment. Swinging the small, drooping figure of the earl into her arms, she led the way out of the kitchen, into the vast, cluttered entrance hall of the mansion. Wending her way cautiously up the sweeping staircase, she directed her little band into one of the huge, musty-smelling bedrooms.

The sight of the massive bed was like a beacon in a storm to the children. Too tired to run, they advanced upon the promise of rest and sleep with single-minded purpose. Hardly waiting for Leslie to sweep off the dusty top coverlet, they climbed solemnly up and settled themselves in a small huddle upon the feathered-packed mattress. Sighs of contentment blended softly with a sneeze from the earl. Tenderly Leslie removed small shoes, gently she wrapped the coverlet over her beloved charges. Then she crept softly out to search for food and water. There would be time enough later in the afternoon to lead a foray upon the hoped-for treasure of clean clothing in the attics.

Chapter 7

Drogo Trevelyan was in a temper. Only those few people who knew him very well could have recognized the subtle signs—the slight narrowing of the golden cat eyes under heavy, drooping lids, the almost imperceptible hardening of the handsome features, the faint white line marking the patrician flare of nostrils. His servants recognized the signs through long familiarity, and behaved with the utmost circumspection.

One cause of the duke's anger was the information he had managed to pick up from the host after dinner the preceding evening. The fellow had come obsequiously into the private dining room, asking if there was anything else he might do to insure His Grace's comfort.

"For we have not seen enough of you these past years, if I may be permitted to say so, Your Grace."

Both of them knew he was overstepping his bounds, but the innkeeper was consumed with curiosity and the duke needed to know more about the Mysterious Purchaser, so the impertinence was permitted.

The facts—as Host Cross related them—were disturbing. It had evidently been an open secret in the county that *someone* was buying up all the free land and any estates or holdings whose owners were willing to sell. It seemed that the only landowners who had *not* been approached were Kenelm and Endale. The duke could have told Cross that an offer had been made to his man-of-law, but he was reluctant to confide in anyone until he had more information. Coolly scanning the red, avid face of the innkeeper, who was now babbling some tale of noble children stolen from their home by gypsies, the duke said blightingly, "I shall be requiring breakfast before nine tomorrow, Cross. You may serve it here."

It had been an adequate breakfast, but Drogo was still angry as he sat in his impressive coach, jolting over the wretched road that led from the village to his estate, and wishing he had thought to bring Muir down to Kenelm with him. His valet, Parsons, might have to be dragooned into acting as secretary if notes needed to be made. The duke cursed himself for not bringing Parsons with him this morning. He fully intended to call upon two or three of the local gentry who had already sold their estates, and the one or two who had refused to do so. Perhaps they might be willing to share any information they had gained as to the Mysterious Buyer.

Just before dawn, wakeful, Drogo had been struck by a curious idea. Muir had informed him of the offer received for Kenelm Place. Which meant that unless Endale had also had an offer that the local gossips were not yet aware of, then the Mysterious Buyer could well be Endale!

A moment's thought had him recalling Muir's mention that the former earl had been killed, leaving a nine-year-old child to assume the title. Obviously *he* would not be attempting secret negotiations to acquire a monopoly of local land. But there had been mention of a guardian, had there not? The whole problem seemed, thought the duke irascibly, to have been expressly and deliberately designed to annoy him. Had it not been for this manipulator, Drogo Trevelyan would happily have passed the rest of his life without thinking once of the home of his detested parent. As it was, he was now being jostled and jolted over what must be the worst-kept roads in England, on his way to enter a door he had sworn never to darken again!

As a way to vent his spleen, Trevelyan took a good deal of pleasure in a brief encounter at the main gates of his ancestral home. The surly custodian, Dawls, routed from his lair in the gate house, did not at first perceive that the impressive vehicle, whose arrogant coachman was vociferously demanding entrance, concealed an occupant in its shadowy interior.

"Bustle about, then, lackwit! Get them gates open on the double, you jolterheaded nincompoop!" bawled the coachman.

Dawls, roused from slumber, did not take kindly to this greeting. He returned an equally vociferous and even ruder refusal.

Tom Coachman's eyes bulged apprehensively as he slanted a glance behind him toward the darkened interior of the carriage, whose heavy window was now being lowered. His cautionary hiss was cut short by the steel-hard contempt in the voice that issued from the shadowed depths.

"You are Dawls? Get the hell off my land and do not come back, or I'll have you thrown in gaol."

The expression on the custodian's face made the coachman and all three grooms bite back laughter. Dawls shambled forward and peered up into the window. Even Drogo, furious at the crashing ineptness of the guardian of his gates, could not resist a grin. He had smoothed it from his face by the time he leaned forward and glared down at the horror-stricken Dawls.

"Me, guv?" Dawls blurted, staring wide-eyed at the ruthless arrogance of the handsome face above him.

"You may open the gates for me before you get the hell off my lands," Drogo conceded, in a tone that revealed his awareness of his own tolerance.

This time the grooms dissolved into laughter, which they vainly tried to keep silent.

Much refreshed by this encounter, the duke was able to witness the deterioration of his estate in silence, if not with equanimity, as they drove through the neglected park. When his groom opened the door and let down the steps of the coach before the massive entrance to Kenelm Place, however, Drogo's lips tightened. *What the devil had possessed the old man, to let their three-hundred-year holding go to ruin?* So it was again a tight-lipped nobleman who allowed the groom to push open the creaking front door for

30

him. The fellow stood aside then. Drogo smiled grimly. From the glimpse he could get of the interior, Kenelm Place had become a hazard to life and limb.

"Go back to the gates," he instructed the groom. "See Dawls off the premises. Go back to the inn and tell Parsons to find someone from the village to replace that idiot at the gate until I decide what I wish to do about this situation." Then, as if reluctant to have shared even this much of his counsel with a servant, the duke turned and strolled into his home.

He stood in the center of the drawing room, beseiged with unhappy memories. There was a look on his handsome face that none of his cronies would have recognized as he absorbed the scents and sights that brought back old hurts and childish griefs. Then, breaking the ancient spell, a series of slight sounds from somewhere above him caught at his attention. *Rats*, was his first scornful analysis of the rustling and squeaking noises. And then he stiffened, and slanted his golden head, the better to hear. For there were now echoes of human voices coming from an upper floor.

Intruders! Scavengers come to ransack the dying mansion! *Ghouls!*

For the first time in his adult life, Drogo Trevelyan admitted to a sense of possessiveness about his family's home—a sense outraged by this dastardly pillage of a place no longer valued by its rightful owners. Gone was the brief vulnerability he had felt; his golden eyes blazed with fury. With the grace, stealth, and lust of a hunting tiger, the duke ran lightly up the stairs in search of the thieves.

Chapter 8

The duke leaped up the massive stairs, silent and sinuous as a jungle cat. When he reached the upper hallway, he paused to locate the source of the noise that had warned him of the presence of intruders in Kenelm Place.

There—it came again. From the attics, a muttering of several voices. They seemed curiously high and light. Gypsy women, perhaps? Breaking into the deserted mansion to steal whatever of value they could lay their dirty hands on? A wide feral grin, completely mirthless, stretched the duke's well-cut lips. Females or not, the scum were about to get a lesson they'd never forget!

As he moved along the hallway to the stairs leading up to the attics, Drogo passed the door to the ducal apartments. It was wide open. Frowning, he was resolving to investigate later, when a series of sounds from inside the bedroom halted him in his tracks. There were several strangling coughs, followed by three gigantic sneezes.

Momentarily frozen with surprise, the duke wondered if the thieves, like vermin, had infested the whole house. Grimly he retraced his steps, briefly regretting the absence of a weapon. Then he noticed and seized a heavy brass candlestick which sat in tarnished magnificence on a boulle side table under a particularly poor picture of his father. Thus armed, he slipped into the bedroom and, with his back to the wall, scanned the terrain.

There was someone in the ducal bed.

But it was a very small figure indeed, and it was huddled

wretchedly within a tangled heap of dusty covers. Lowering the candlestick, Drogo advanced upon the interloper.

Blue eyes stared up at him from a small white face, and a hoarse little voice croaked valiantly, "May I know why you are invading my bedroom, sir?"

Unfortunately, the boy sneezed again, rather spoiling the effect of his challenge.

The duke found himself grinning. "You may know why I am invading this room when you explain to me your right to be here yourself," he advised grimly. The child did not sound like a gypsy, managing, in spite of his sore throat, to speak with a cultured accent. It was difficult in the dim light—for the heavy drapes were drawn against the sun—to tell exactly what the child looked like, his most impressive feature at the moment being a red, swollen nose.

A little puzzled at the sharpness of his anger at this unwarranted intrusion into the home he himself had vowed never to reenter, Drogo set his countenance in its habitual expression of cold arrogance.

"Give your name at once, boy, and state your reasons for breaking into this house!"

"I'm sorry, sir," the child gasped. "I think I am going to be sick!" He leaned over to grab at a basin placed conveniently upon the floor by the side of the bed.

A few stressful moments later, the duke found himself wiping the pale little face with a damp cloth he found in a dish on the table near the bed. Even while he ministered to the boy, he was fuming at his own gullibility. Why didn't he throw the little thief through the window? Or shake the truth out of him? *An unequal contest, Trevelyan,* he mocked himself. The little intruder really couldn't stop you, whatever you chose to do to him!

But his companions, still happily scavenging the mansion, might prove worthier antagonists, Drogo decided. Far more satisfying to vent his anger upon several adults than on this miserable scrap. What were the boy's parents thinking of? He was already moving along the hallway to the attic stairs, painfully eager to find a physical release for his anger. There was no sound coming from the attics now, and Drogo wondered if his own challenge to the sick child had been overheard. Were the thieves waiting to attack him as he reached the upper floor? He snatched up another candlestick and crept up the narrow stairway.

As he neared the top, he hesitated, listening intently. There came to his ears a low voice, probably female, which seemed to be asking a question. The duke stepped lightly out into the open space.

The first thing presented to his astounded vision was a small but very shapely feminine rear, modestly draped in a mud-spattered skirt. The body was bent over a large, open trunk, obviously taking something from the interior. The duke had his mouth open to roar a challenge, when he was further amazed to behold not one, but two heads in enormous, once fashionable feathered hats rising slowly from behind another big box. A closer look revealed that the absurd hats crowned the heads of two young girls, both of whom were staring at the huge male intruder with horrified alarm.

"*Leslie!*" gasped the taller of the two. "We are discovered! By a MAN!"

"Oh, Hilary, must you be so dramatic?" replied a weary voice from the interior of the trunk. "It's probably a suit of armor."

The second girl gulped and then said clearly, "No, Leslie. For once Hilary is right. I'm afraid the owner of this . . . uh . . . building has caught us—"

"In the act!" interjected Hilary, not to be done out of her sensational announcement. "He looks *very* angry, Leslie."

There was a scramble of movement which, even in that charged moment, Drogo acknowledged to be graceful, and a tall young woman pulled herself up from the trunk and whirled to face him.

He was not impressed by the appearance of the gypsy ringleader. She was dirty, dressed in a frumpish gown, and pale with exhaustion and alarm. Great blue eyes stared at him out of a thick fringe of black lashes. Drogo lowered the candlestick, which he had forgotten until this moment.

When a quick glance around the shadowy expanse of the attics failed to disclose any male intruders, he allowed his vigilance to relax slightly.

"Perhaps you would like to tell me what the devil you are doing rifling through my possessions?" he demanded icily. "I am Kenelm, and this house belongs to me."

The chit surprised him. "Then you are a bad landlord," she snapped. "The estate has been allowed to fall into ruin—a disgrace to the neighborhood! Since the old duke is dead, you must be his son. Why did you not return for his funeral?" She glared at him in a very minatory fashion.

This impudence, on top of her own nefarious and quite indefensible actions, served to revive the fury that Drogo had been trying to repress for the last forty-eight hours— ever since, in fact, he had realized that he would have to return to the scene of his youthful misery and disillusionment.

Setting his jaw, the duke prepared to demolish this saucy interloper.

"You will all accompany me downstairs, where my groom will escort you to the local constable."

Even in his anger, the duke now became aware of the sick horror that filled the faces of all three girls. *Aha, they are guilty of more than a little theft!* was his first deduction. *Or perhaps the knowledge that the punishment for theft is transportation was enough to put the fear into the little trollops.* Drogo took a closer look.

Decked out in those ridiculous hats, the girls did not have the appearance of gypsies or criminals. In fact, they were actually rather an attractive trio, albeit obviously not at their best at the moment. And their speech was as cultured as the boy's. *The boy's—* Light dawned.

"Do I take it I am addressing the sisters of the new Earl of Endale?" asked Drogo in a hatefully cold voice. "The irresponsible brats whose exploits are the talk of the county? Whose greatly-to-be-pitied guardian has been scouring the woods and fields in search of your murdered bodies?"

"Is that the story he is spreading?" asked the oldest girl.

"Clever of him! If he had found us, I am sure we *would* have been discovered . . . murdered."

There was an odd silence. Neither of the other two little females seemed surprised at this monstrous suggestion. "You are saying he would have killed you if he had found you?" sneered the duke. "Has your behavior been such that you deserve it?"

Oddly enough, it was the youngest of the girls who answered him in a sober little voice. "Cousin March keeps telling everyone how ungrateful and naughty we are, and when the horse threw Daryl, he tried to make it out an accident, and then when Daryl's room caught fire, and Leslie saved him, Cousin March said Daryl had lit the fire himself! As if anyone would be so foolish!" The girl stepped out from behind the huge box and advanced soberly toward him. "I am Meredith," she said with incongruous formality. "And this is my older sister Hilary," indicating the pretty child who had announced his arrival so dramatically. "Hilary is emotional," she explained kindly. "And this is our oldest sister, Leslie. She is taking us to seek shelter with our father's great-aunt, Lady Bella Endale. It was Leslie who led us safely through the woods at night to this empty house where we could wait hidden for the London coach."

Drogo Trevelyan stared at the pale-faced, huge-eyed young woman. What was the matter with the chit? Did she have nothing to say for herself? "Your brother is very ill," he said coldly. "Do you think it sensible to expose a sick child to such hazards?"

Leslie tried to pull together her disordered wits. Since she first set eyes upon this huge, handsome male creature, she had not been able to think coherently. He was the most beautiful human being she had ever met. She could not seem to drag her eyes away from his magnificent figure, set off so well in an elegant riding coat, skintight buckskins, and polished Hessian boots. After one glance at his face, she had not dared to look again into eyes that gleamed like golden gems in the handsome countenance. But it was more than his stunning beauty that held her silent.

It was the sudden strange, almost frightening knowledge that this man was important to her—possibly more important than any human being she had ever met. She had felt the oddest sense of *recognition* when she met those narrowed, catlike golden eyes, a sense almost of *homecoming*. But the icy arrogance, the cold, sneering dislike in his deep voice told her very definitely that her sense of kinship—or whatever it was—was not reciprocated. Not only did His Grace the duke not experience any sense of recognition, he very plainly felt a need to be rid of her and her family as quickly as possible!

Yet something very deeply rooted within Leslie informed her that she must not allow her little party to be shuffled off. Her own remarkable response to the big man aside, Daryl must not be exposed again to the terrible threat of March Wardell's control. Some plan would have to be worked out, some delaying action put in motion. . . .

Oddly enough, it was the overdramatic, insecure Hilary who provided a temporary respite.

"Oh, gods! I think I am going to faint!" she gasped, her chalk-white face giving credence to the cry.

And she sank to the dusty attic floor, the ridiculous bonnet falling forward over her ashen countenance.

"Now see what you have done!" scolded Meredith, with a stern look at the duke. "Have you no sense at all? We haven't eaten for two days, and we're cold and wretched and terrified of our greedy, cruel cousin—and you frightened poor Hilary out of her wits! Are you just going to let her lie there, you insensitive man?"

Gritting his teeth, the duke bent and lifted the inert girl in his arms. "If you will precede me down those rather narrow stairs," he hissed, "I will get the child—" he glared down at the pale, still face at his shoulder "—the *girl* down to one of the bedrooms, where I am sure you will be able to revive her." This last was ground out with such a wealth of suspicion that Leslie, oddly happy at the turn of events, was forced to smother a smile.

"The state of Your Grace's residence is hardly such as

to provide ease and succor for an unconscious female,'' she said provocatively.

The duke, who had reached the bottom of the stairway with his burden, cast her a resentful look. Striding along the wide hall toward his mother's old bedroom, he snapped, ''Since I was not informed that I should be entertaining *guests*, I believe I may be forgiven for the state of the accommodations—''

''Oh,'' said Leslie, daring greatly, ''is this the style of accommodation you normally prefer?''

There ensued a silence that no one cared to break.

As he deposited the still inert form upon the bed that had been his mama's, the duke said shortly, ''What is wrong with her? Or do you care enough to find out?''

''She is, as Meredith mentioned, weary, hungry, and chilled to the bone. But above all, she is doing her best to fight off the fear we all have—that our greedy cousin March Wardell, my brother's heir, will finish the job he has already attempted twice. To murder Endale,'' Leslie stated quietly. And then: ''I claim sanctuary under your shield, Kenelm.''

The sheer audacity of the claim, as much as its medieval quaintness, held the duke silent for a moment. He stared hard into the girl's face, seeking a sign of guile or mockery. There was none. The huge, remarkable deep blue eyes seemed to glow with light in the sweet, pale face; the dainty jaw was set courageously against mockery or rejection. When Drogo found himself queerly unable to respond, the slender shoulders squared in grim acceptance of the burden.

''Will you then grant us the favor of a chance to shelter here until the earl is strong enough to be taken to London to Lady Bella, Your Grace?'' Leslie urged. ''It cannot hurt you to permit us the shelter of this wretched, unwanted estate of yours. And I swear to you, as God is my witness, that March Wardell means to destroy my brother.''

Then, lovely eyes steady upon his own, the girl stood waiting for the duke's answer.

Chapter 9

Tawny golden eyes as fiercely intent as any predator's held and challenged wide, steady blue ones. For an endless moment, the duke made no reply to Leslie's appeal. And then the coldest smile she had ever seen curved the well-cut lips.

"So you claim sanctuary of Kenelm, do you, my dear?" asked Drogo Trevelyan, that gazetted rakehell. There was a note in his voice that sent a chill along Leslie's nerves. Before she could answer his question, he went on, too smoothly, "It might amuse me to set you up in a cozy little establishment. . . ." He paused, his smile infinitely suggestive.

Meredith uttered a crow of delight. "Leslie! You've done the thing! You promised you would bring us safely out of this terrible dilemma—and you have!" She turned to the duke with a wide, childish smile. "We shall all be forever in your debt, Your Grace! Chivalry is not dead!"

The duke was too startled by this gushing effusiveness to notice the look of shocked surprise on Leslie's face at the very uncharacteristic behavior of steady, sensible Meredith. And then Hilary, now revived and unwilling to be overshadowed by her younger sister, addressed the startled duke with her own flow of emotional gratitude.

"*Our own establishment!* How superbly generous of Your Grace! But of course it will not do! We must stay with our Great-aunt Endale! We could not permit the quizzies to misconstrue your generous offer!"

The duke, for once in his suavely sophisticated life at a complete loss, turned a bewildered countenance toward Leslie. Surely her sisters could not be quite so naive? his elevated eyebrows seemed to ask. And then suspicion drew those tawny bars down in a frown. Or were they already smart and sly enough to seize an advantage? Was this social gush a *ploy*? The man's face darkened with angry color. Did they learn it in their cradles?

"If you Endale women are trying to chouse me," he said crudely. "I warn you, you'll catch cold at it!"

Leslie forced herself out of the strange enchantment that had held her since first she set eyes on this beautiful, wicked male. Trying to present a serene front, she said softly, "My sisters are merely expressing gratitude for the . . . ah . . . most *generous* offer of assistance which you have graciously made us. Our governess, Miss Wheaton, taught us always to acknowledge kindness. Now will you be good enough to explain in what way we are trying to—I believe *chouse you* was the term?" She smiled with adorable sweetness at the lowering nobleman. "What does it mean, chouse?"

For a long moment the duke said nothing. Then a light began to glow in his eyes, and a reluctant grin tugged at his lips.

"Oh, yes, Madame Prim and Proper! Of course you know nothing of robbing a gentleman's house!" He grinned at the two younger girls. "You Endales choose to commit your larcenies in style, do you not? Such elaborate bonnets for a bit of pilfering!"

"Of course you know these hats belong to you—" began Meredith stiffly.

"Surely not *to me*," goaded their tormentor.

"To your family, I meant," persisted Meredith doggedly. "We—I could not resist trying them on." She straightened the absurd creation on her small head, and cocked it naughtily. "*A la mode*, is it not?" She smiled up at the big, awesomely handsome male.

Drogo was betrayed into a bark of laughter at the ridiculous appearance the three females presented. If they were in truth thieves, they were the most absurd and colorful he had ever encountered.

And if they were in truth sisters of the Earl of Endale? The question triggered off a memory of the small, wretchedly uncomfortable little boy. Irrationally, the duke blamed the child's sisters for his own neglect. He stared at the girls with his most forbidding expression.

"Do you intend to leave the boy alone to suffer his pain?" he inquired ruthlessly. "He was very sick when I left him."

This taunt was accepted by the earl's sisters with stricken looks. Leslie roused herself into action, casting off the strange paralysis that had held her since she first set eyes upon His Grace. Without a word, she turned and ran lightly out of the bedroom and along the wide hallway to the room in which she had left her brother. He was still there in the rumpled bed, breathing heavily in his troubled sleep.

She was bending over him, her hand on his hot forehead, when her sisters and the duke came into the room. Leslie lifted an anxious countenance to greet them.

"Is he worse?" demanded Hilary, before anyone else could speak. "Oh, Leslie, is he . . . *dying*?"

"Of course not," retorted Leslie prosaically. "He has a very bad inflammation of the nose and throat, that is all."

"You are trained as a physician?" challenged the duke snidely.

Her impatient glare seemed to amuse him.

Again Meredith played mediator. "Hilary tends to find tragedy at every turn," she explained to their cruelly smiling host. Ignoring her sister's sullen pout, she went on gravely, "We really are very grateful for your compassion, sir. We are all so weary from our trip through the woods to this refuge! Leslie hardly slept at all. She was watching over us, protecting us—"

"Having first plunged you all into an impossible situation with her childish fears," added the duke blightingly, "protecting you seems the least she could do."

This last, unjust attack roused Leslie from her strange bemusement with this arrogant nobleman. Narrowing her lids over her wide blue eyes, she said coldly, "You know nothing of the events which led to my decision. No rational man could expect me to leave the earl where his life was in danger." She glanced down at the sleeping child. "If you can bear to let us remain in your . . . home until to-morrow morning, I promise we shall not trouble you further."

For some reason, this displeased the duke.

"You can promise that the boy will be well enough to travel by that time?" challenged the nobleman.

Leslie bit back a rude retort. "I shall try to make other arrangements," she answered wearily.

"You are a fool," said the duke callously. "I shall not permit you to subject the Earl of Endale to any more totty-headed starts. Creeping through the woods at night! Getting these children soaked to the skin, and then forcing them to sleep in their wet garments! It is God's mercy they are not all dead of pneumonia!"

This vicious attack silenced all three girls. Leslie, racked with guilt, could not face the duke's condemnation, but peered fearfully into the frightened countenances of her sisters.

Hilary sobbed once, loudly. "What were we to do, sir?" she demanded. "Our cousin has tried to kill Endale by putting him up on a savage horse and then striking the animal with his crop! And that very night, there was a fire in Daryl's bedroom, which might have burned him as he slept! Would you have us leave our brother in that place of danger and death?" Her rather theatrical challenge did not, as Leslie feared, put an end to the duke's fragile patience. He stared moodily at his uninvited female guests for a long moment, and then looked down at the restless sleeper. He seemed to come to a decision.

"You say you are heading for London, and Lady Endale? I know the ancient beldame, and I warn you now, you can expect very little assistance, if any, from that selfish old female. However, it is plain I cannot leave you here." He halted Leslie's objections with an arrogant, uplifted palm. "It would furnish a bad precedent if every hedge-bird who wished to do so got the idea he could enter and despoil Kenelm Place at his whim. So I shall bundle up my fellow nobleman, carry him down to my carriage, and stow you all out of sight on the floor until we are safely away from the village.''

There was a chorus of thanks and fulsome admiration from the two younger girls, Hilary even going so far as to name the duke their Benefactor, to Leslie's annoyance. Older and a little wiser than her sisters, she was sure there was a predatory gleam in the Benefactor's tawny eyes, a light that boded ill for one at least of the orphans. She looked up to find that daunting gaze resting upon her with a very *knowing* expression.

The duke favored Leslie with a slow, devastating smile.

''I'm sure we shall think of some way you can repay me for my extreme kindness,'' he said softly.

Chapter 10

In point of fact, Drogo Trevelyan had surprised himself by his response to the invading females. He had been well taught—first by a mama who was a self-indulgent, bitterly dissatisfied hypochondriac, later by a series of ladies, some wellborn, some gutter bred, all of whom had proved to be greedy, unscrupulous light-o'-loves. He thought he had learned his lesson well: to invest neither trust nor affection in any woman, however beautiful, however appealing to his senses.

But these absurd little ragamuffins, grimy and dowdy though they were, had somehow caused him to abandon, if only temporarily, his hard-won wisdom. It shocked him that he had not summarily turned them over to the village constable, as he had every intention of doing. Worse, he had as good as pledged himself to deliver the brats to their irascible, niffy-naffy Great-aunt Endale—who would not thank him for the favor!

Thinking of the old battle-ax, Drogo grinned involuntarily. He almost wished he might be present during the first encounter of the aged beldame and her unconventional relatives! But no! Not even for the laugh such a farce might provide would he trouble himself one second longer than necessary with the encroaching females!

There was, of course, the small matter of the payment he intended to exact from the oldest girl, the curiously silent Leslie. Some evening during the trip, when the younger children were safely settled in the bedchamber he would provide for them, he intended to summon Leslie to his own room and discover at his leisure just what it was about her that piqued his notoriously jaded interest. Claim sanctuary, would she? They would see about that! For a moment the duke felt the oddest twinge of some emotion he did not recognize. Frowning, he decided that it must be his reluctance to be seen in any public place with the grimy little females. So first get them hidden in his carriage and on the road to London, then stop in the next sizable town and purchase for them all some clothing that would not shame their . . . protector.

With a wicked grin, the duke decided he was well enough satisfied with his plan. Endale was too young to enter a protest, whatever his "Benefactor" did, and the younger girls, for all their dramatics, were powerless. As for the oldest sister—pale, weary Leslie of the huge blue eyes and the bewitching smile—Drogo Trevelyan had handled more difficult ladybirds!

Feeling much more himself, the duke ordered the girls to bring bedcovers under which they might conceal themselves in the carriage, and to wrap their little brother in a sheet and two blankets so that he might be as comfortable as possible on the trip.

"Do you wish me to bring Endale down to your carriage now, Your Grace?" asked the oldest girl tonelessly. Drogo was pleased that she did not meet his eyes as she spoke. It would appear that he had quelled her impudent attempts at defiance. Well, quelled or not, he'd soon have her dancing to his tune—one way or another! Announcing that he would send a groom to carry the boy, the duke ran lightly down the great staircase, summoned his coachman, and gave orders that the carriage was to be prepared at once to receive visitors.

"We shall not be returning to the Kenelm Arms tonight, Tom," Drogo said briskly. "You will stop there only long enough to give Parsons my orders to pack my things, pay the landlord, and follow us in a hired coach to the inn we stopped at on our way here."

If he was surprised at this fresh start of his master's,

Tom Coachman gave no sign of it. His nod of assent seemed to indicate that *no* rig Kenelm could run would ever surprise *him*!

Still, the duke fixed him with a cold stare.

"You will advise your fellow servants that nothing—and I mean *nothing*—is to be said of any persons we have encountered in Kenelm Place, or that we may be transporting to London."

The duke's golden eyes were so cold that Tom Coachman nodded much more vigorously and even ventured a "Yes, 'ndeed, Yer Grace, mum's the word!" in a placating tone.

With a last minatory glare, the duke turned and strode back up the stairs.

The trip to the Hart and Hound Inn was a nightmare for the Endales. The earl seemed to be drifting in and out of a fretful slumber. His sisters did their anguished best to make him comfortable, but it was almost impossible, given their situation. During the ride to the Kenelm Arms and for a good half hour after the carriage had driven away from the village, the duke insisted upon the four young people remaining under the covering the groom and coachman had arranged over them within the carriage. It was hideously uncomfortable for them, nested on the floor in the space between the front and rear-facing seats of the elegant vehicle. None of the girls wished to complain, however, since they were, in fact, achieving their devoutly desired goal: to escape to London without alerting March Wardell to their presence or their destination.

After an interminable time the duke ordered the carriage to a halt. Bending over, he lifted one edge of the cover, and in a tone Leslie found insufferably smug, he announced, "You may sit up now. I have succeeded in getting you away without letting the . . . ah . . . cat out of the bag."

Fury flamed up in Leslie's eyes. "You are *enjoying* this, are you not, sir?" Of course he was, sitting cool and comfortable against the luxurious upholstery of the carriage squabs while the Endales smothered beneath his dusty covers!

His knowing grin did nothing to assuage her wrath. "Is this the thanks your Benefactor is to receive for his selfless, warmhearted efforts in your behalf?" he asked, in a fashionably fading voice—and then spoiled the effect by breaking into a wicked chuckle.

"I hate you," said Leslie quietly, cradling Daryl against her breast.

"Of course you do," agreed the hateful creature with a grin. "All recipients of charity hate their Benefactors."

Although lightly spoken, the comment gave Leslie pause. Did she, indeed, resent the fact that the duke was able to rescue her family when she could not? Was it false pride that roused in her breast this powerful emotion toward Drogo Trevelyan? She lifted wide blue eyes to the man's challenging stare. And then she surprised him.

"I beg your pardon," she said with absolute sincerity. "I have been at fault, resenting your wonderful assistance. It is only"—she tried to explain her paltry behavior—"that I had expected—hoped—to save my brother and sisters myself. I stand corrected, sir. We are in your hands."

Drogo felt as though he had received a wisty blow to the solar plexus. Never in his admittedly wide social experience had any woman ever come out so frankly with an acknowledgment of her own failings. Was she sincere? Impossible to doubt it, with those wide, honest blue eyes open to her very soul! With a frisson of . . . *alarm*? Drogo realized that he was dealing with a different kind of female in this little creature. A *rara avis*, a strange prodigy: a totally honest woman! He subjected the girl to a frowning scrutiny, which she bore quietly.

"Look after your brother," he snapped finally. "There is water and a moist cloth in that basket."

A long, silent time later (for the younger girls were too weary and anxious to chatter), the carriage drew up in a cobbled yard, and Tom Coachman loudly demanded stabling for his team, and servants to attend his master.

While the bustle of welcome was building outside the

47

carriage, the duke leaned forward, surveyed his disheveled guests disparagingly, and said to Leslie, "You will remain silent within the coach until my servants come to bring you into the inn—through a side door, I hope! You are such grimy creatures! I shall have to fabricate some plausible story to explain the presence of four little urchins under my shield. . . ." His mouth twitched.

He is amused by our plight! thought Leslie, setting her teeth against the rage that his offhand attitude was again rousing in her. *One day, when we are safe, Kenelm—!*

Meanwhile, it was only sensible to do as the arrogant creature ordered.

"My brother—" she began, the words seeming to rasp out of her burning throat.

"I shall send for a doctor at once," said the duke in a kinder voice than he had yet used.

Whatever his ultimate intentions, it was no plan of Drogo's to torment the runaways. Within a half hour he had the girls established in a large, comfortable bedroom, and the little earl in a smaller room which opened off theirs. Plenty of hot water and clean towels appeared shortly thereafter, brought by two smiling maids, and His Grace's valet delivered a bar of pleasant-smelling soap and a comb and brush. Leslie decided these latter had come from His Grace's luggage, since the soap was very fine, French, and most seductively scented. Leslie shivered as she stroked it onto her relaxing body in one of the two tubs the landlord had provided. She dried and dressed herself quickly, anxious to check on her brother's condition.

She had already bathed Daryl, and given him all the fresh water he wished to drink. Now he was comfortably tucked into a small bed, already relaxed and looking better.

"We are safe now, aren't we, Leslie?" he whispered, reaching up to cling to the gentle hand that was stroking his head.

Leslie smiled encouragingly. "Yes, Daryl, we are safe, thanks to our kind Benefactor, the Duke of Kenelm," she said softly. "He has agreed to support a fellow nobleman,

48

and see us safe to Great-aunt Bella," she added, with her sweet smile.

"I am glad you recognize my . . . ah . . . nobility," came a hatefully soft voice at her shoulder. "Here is Dr. Gregory to deal with your brother's illness."

Leslie went out into the room she shared with her sisters, more than a little relieved by the arrangements the arrogant duke had made. Perhaps it was the fashion in London to speak so . . . suggestively to a female as he had done to her. She was probably a provincial little prude to read sensual challenges into so many of the casual remarks the man made. Sighing, Leslie accepted the enthusiastic invitation of her sisters to sit down at the table and partake of the delicious repast the innkeeper had provided.

For a space of time there was no conversation as the girls assuaged several days' hunger. Then Meredith, voicing all their hidden fears, and as ever, honest enough to face them, whispered, "Is Daryl going to recover soon?"

"We shall have to wait to hear what Dr. Gregory has to tell us," Leslie answered. "I am sure he will know exactly what to do for the best for Daryl."

Their anxiety was relieved a few minutes later when the doctor came out of the sickroom with a reassuring verdict. Although the boy's illness sounded and looked serious, it was actually no more than a putrid sore throat, and would yield to treatment within a day or so.

"Your brother is a sturdy little fellow. Keep him quiet for a day or so, plenty of water to drink and as much food as he cares for, and he will be right as rain."

Accepting their thanks, he nodded when the duke gave him some folded bank notes.

When he had left, Leslie, who had noted the transfer of money with chagrin, asked if she might have a few moments of His Grace's time. "In private, if you please," she added quietly.

The duke's eyebrows rose slightly, and then a smile

twisted at his lips. "But of course, Lady Leslie," he said softly. "I am free now." He preceded her from the room.

With a quick word or two to her sisters, and a reassuring smile, Leslie hurried after the arrogant nobleman. *He could have had the kindness to wait for her, rather than striding along the hallway ahead of her like a—an Eastern potentate with his slave!* Under her smoldering gaze, the big man turned into a doorway near the front of the building. Well, at least he had the decency to get us rooms that did not connect with his! she thought. Perhaps he is not so bad as I imagined. It cannot have been any great pleasure to him to have to accept responsibility for a whole family of refugees! With a much more tolerant attitude toward their prickly Benefactor, Leslie followed his broad back into the room, heard the door close sharply—and found herself in his arms!

Chapter 11

Whatever response Drogo had expected—and he was prepared, he thought smugly, for anything from terrified missishness to delighted cooperation—he was, in the event, completely surprised by Leslie's behavior. The girl stood quietly within his light clasp, staring up at his mocking smile with wide blue eyes that neither pleaded nor coaxed. In point of fact, the maddening little chit seemed to be assessing him in the same cool way he himself often appraised a female whom he considered honoring with his attentions. It was a new and unflattering experience.

Annoyed, His Grace tightened his grip.

This brought an unexpected reaction. The girl pulled back a little from his embrace. "Excuse me, please. There is something I must . . ." Her slender fingers were working at the inside of her bodice.

Fascinated, Drogo released his grip and moved slightly away from the tall, slender figure, giving her room to work. Whatever was the little female up to? His eyes sparkled with interest. And then widened with shock. For, as he watched, Leslie unpinned a small silk reticule and pulled it from her bodice.

Opening it to disclose some guineas, she said firmly, "If you will tell me the amount you paid the doctor for his attendance upon Daryl, I shall recompense you. Endale provides for its own."

Strangely affronted, Drogo gave the presumptuous girl a

51

sneering smile. "You intend to provide for a sick child with those paltry coins? Where did you *pick them up*?"

"They were love gifts from my father on happy occasions in the past. How much do we owe you, Kenelm?" The bleak look upon the girl's face struck Drogo so sharply that he hit back without thinking.

"You insult me!"

"As you do me," retorted the unnatural female without heat.

It was her calm, remote air that infuriated the nobleman beyond bearing. What right had this little chit to bandy words with him, or, when it came to that, to refuse his generously offered aid so cavalierly? It became clear to the duke that this unnatural female needed a sharp set-down. Or, better, a course of instruction in social graces, which, somehow, must be administered by himself.

This odd conclusion so startled His Grace that he did not hear the chit's next remark, which she repeated, in tones of maddening condescension. "Your Grace! I must return to my family at once. If you will tell me the sum you expended on Daryl's care, I shall give your valet the amount, thus sparing your . . . delicate sensibilities."

By the gods! Was the female laughing at him? Drogo was swept with such a fury of unusual emotions that for a few seconds he could not make his throat function. When finally he had found his voice, he snapped out the first insult he could think of. "You think to repay me with a few coins for rescuing you from the wretched imbroglio you yourself created? For disrupting all my plans to restore my family's home, in order to snatch you away clandestinely from a no doubt rightfully angered guardian? I should have left you there to be caught and dragged publicly back to your own home!"

The effect of this diatribe was far greater than he might have expected. Leslie's face whitened with shock and guilt. "Your plans . . . ?" she repeated. "But I had no idea you cared what happened to Kenelm Place! Everyone said you wanted it to fall to ruin!"

Ignoring the fact that everyone had been, in this case,

absolutely correct, Drogo said sharply, "Just as *everyone says* that your guardian is an admirable, long-suffering saint to put up with the insolent behavior of you spoilt children!"

The girl seemed to have herself in control now, although her face was still pale and anxious. "I did not know," she murmured, distractedly. "When I claimed sanctuary, I had no idea you were intending to restore your home to its former magnificence. Please forgive me, Your Grace. Of course we shall go on to London by stagecoach tomorrow." She drew a deep breath, which pulled the man's eyes involuntarily to her tender young breast. "We are forever in your debt for your gallant rescue of a set of troublesome brats, sir. Only let me assure you I was not lying when I told you of Wardell's actions against the earl. Daryl will be safe, I think, with our great-aunt." She made a graceful curtsy. "Again, Endale's thanks, Your Grace! We shall never forget your kindness."

As she turned to open the door, Drogo was cursing himself for a bungler. It was not like him to move so awkwardly in pursuit, but this little bird was no ordinary quarry. Why did he bother? She was not strikingly beautiful, aside from those remarkable eyes. She was certainly not eager for his advances! Let her go, Kenelm, she's trouble! he advised himself.

All of which sage and sensible advice did not prevent him from striding forward and seizing the little enigma by one shoulder as she opened the door. "We have not finished our business," he said gruffly, in response to her surprised look. "I think my sensibilites are sufficiently— *indelicate* to endure a businesslike settlement. Now."

He pulled her ruthlessly back into the room and shut the door again. "I believe we had better seat ourselves. This may take time."

"Can it not be handled in the morning, sir? I am . . . very anxious about my family."

"Now," said the duke decisively. Then, for the life of him unable to think of a proper way to inform the girl that she was to serve as his mistress for a short period in repayment for his generosity, he allowed himself a time-making diversion. "We shall have a glass of brandy—that is, you do drink brandy, I presume?"

Leslie's spontaneous, naughty grin startled him. "I have been known to," she admitted. "I am almost eighteen, after all, and the daughter of an acknowledged connoisseur."

Then, taking pity on his obvious surprise, she added, "I took a small clay bottleful to warm and soothe us during our flight."

"You gave those children brandy?" he heard himself exclaim.

"And myself. I believe it was all that saved us, during those long, cold days hiding in the damp woods," the girl replied.

Drogo found he was speaking through clenched teeth. "I suppose you did not stop to consider just what that ill-judged tippling might have led to?" Conscious that his voice was rising, Drogo restrained himself from delivering the lecture he ached to impart to the little idiot. "You need a keeper," he snapped.

"Is that your *business*, Kenelm? To offer me the dubious honor of your . . . patronage? I hardly think such an action on my part would endear Lady Bella to the idea of sponsoring my sisters and the earl. Like Caesar's wife, Endale's sister must be above reproach!"

Drogo felt as though he had received a stunning, unexpected blow. Hell and damnation, had he actually offered to take the little fool under his protection, knowing who and *what* she was? The little witch had him on a roundabout, off balance!

"I must be mad," he muttered.

Leslie laughed. "On that point, we agree," she said softly. "Now let us both be sensible, wish one another well, and say good night, before either of us has a chance to do anything silly." She rose and stood close to him, offering her hand with a friendly smile.

Drogo took it. Slowly he raised it to his lips.

"You smell of sandalwood," he found himself murmuring.

"Your soap," agreed the girl. "It's delightful! I shall think of you every time I smell it."

The duke straightened his fine body and grinned ruefully down at the saucy little chit.

"I think we had better get that 'good night' said before I am tempted to wring your pretty little neck," he quipped.

Leslie whipped out the door so smartly that the duke was forced to grin. Clearly he was not the only one affected!

It was probably a good thing that he'd never have to meet the little wench again!

Chapter 12

Of course, he was wrong.

A moment's rational thought convinced him that, having been gulled into giving his protection, however reluctantly, to the clutch of little orphans, he was now obligated to see them safely to their great-aunt's residence in London. A Trevelyan could not draw back, having once committed himself!

Committed is the right word, the duke thought wryly. *And Bedlam is the place!* However had the little Leslie succeeded where so many of her sex had failed? It seemed he was compelled to sponsor the Endales whether they—or he himself—liked it or not.

So be it. The first order of business was to produce clothing for them that would not be a public shame to him. Summoning Parsons, who was eaten up by curiosity about his master's uncharacteristic behavior, the duke gave concise orders.

"These children we are convoying to London are the Earl of Endale and his sisters. They tell me they are running away from a wicked guardian." His saturnine expression revealed exactly what he thought about *that* story. "Their destination, however, is unexceptionable: the home of Lady Bella Endale, their great-aunt. In spite of the fact that I am under obligation to their recently deceased father," (a convenient fiction) "I cannot permit myself to be embarrassed in public by their ragamuffin appearance. Therefore you will secure new, clean clothes for the earl.

Since he is confined to his bed, you may take his old garments to be sure of the sizes. Spare no expense."

Parsons was so pleased at being, at last, *in the know* that he ventured a question. "And the . . . young ladies, Your Grace?"

The duke breathed out an elaborate sigh, which did not deceive his longtime servant for an instant. "I suppose we must furbish up the little females, also," he conceded. "Do your best, Parsons. I have every confidence in you."

The two worldly-wise males exchanged a glance, and Parsons plunged at once into his fascinating assignment. He was an acknowledged genius in the skills it took to turn out his master as a nonpareil, yet secretly he had longed to experiment in dressing less elegant figures. The little Endales would be an exciting challenge! Especially, he thought, the oldest girl. That little filly had all the marks of a *dark horse*! Parsons was not sure if the duke realized just what he had caught—or perhaps, the valet amended with a secret grin, what had caught him! That idea so tickled the normally austere Parsons that he indulged in a rare flight of fancy: the possibility of creating a diamond—or at least a charmer—from the material at hand. Now *that* would be a real challenge!

By the time Parsons returned from his sortie into the local emporia, the duke was in a nasty temper. His heavy eyelids were narrowed over smoldering amber eyes (always a bad sign), and his well-cut lips were set in a tight, straight line. He greeted his valet with a snarl.

"Where have you been? I have had the devil of a time keeping these little ingrates from rushing off to London in rags which would dishonor their hostess—*if* her butler ever permitted them to enter the house!"

Parsons regarded the set, stubborn countenance of Leslie, and the solemn, apprehensive expressions of Hilary and Meredith. The girls were seated in a prim row on a sofa in the duke's sitting room. A smile tugged at the corners of the valet's mouth, but his tone was blandly confident as he remarked, "I am sure you young ladies will express proper gratitude to your Benefactor when you see

57

the smart and suitable clothing he has provided for you in which to meet Lady Bella.'' Irresistibly reminding the girls of Miss Wheaton at her most minatory, his glance rested on their obviously tatterdemalion attire. Quite ignoring the horrendous frown that now appeared on Leslie's face, he continued calmly, ''I hear from the innkeeper that the doctor has said the earl will be well enough to resume the journey by tomorrow. Perhaps you might wish to take your sisters to your room now, milady, and inspect the garments which have been procured for you?''

He asked it as a question, but every person in the room knew it was as good as a command. Leslie rose with what aplomb she could collect, and led her silent sisters out of the duke's sitting room.

''Well done, Parsons,'' said the duke morosely, as soon as the door had closed behind his reluctant guests. ''We had just been having the devil of a disagreement. *Women*!''

''Indeed, Your Grace,'' Parsons soothed. ''They are kittle-cattle at best.''

The duke snorted a humorless laugh. It was not his custom to discuss private matters with his valet, but the fellow always seemed to know everything that was happening anyway, and since he seldom ventured to make a comment, the duke accepted his omniscience as a characteristic of a good servant. Upon this occasion, however, His Grace felt the need of all the advice he could get.

Glaring balefully at the blameless valet, he said harshly, ''She insists she must take the *stagecoach* as soon as the boy is able to travel.''

''Quite ineligible,'' Parsons said firmly.

The duke's expression lightened. ''She stated that she would not wear any garments of my providing,'' continued the insulted Benefactor.

''Wait until she and those sisters of hers see what is in the boxes,'' advised Parsons smugly.

''She is determined to pay me back for any monies I have expended upon her.''

This piece of information quite shocked the valet. He pondered the matter for a few moments. Then, triumphantly, he assured his master, "Lady Bella will soon put that nonsense out of her head. If you could put the young lady off—very gently, of course!—until you deposit her safely with her relative. . . .?" His eyebrows rose in a conspiratorial fashion, which immediately pulled Drogo out of his bad temper.

"You are a Machiavelli, Parsons," he grinned. "But then, it is so much simpler to be the one who suggests these skillful ploys than the one who has to carry them out!"

Good humor restored, the duke strode from the room to take a refreshing amble through the little town, whose name he had not bothered to learn. Gazing with restrained admiration after the well-set-up, elegantly dressed figure, Parsons permitted himself a small smile. Not too difficult to handle, he thought, if one knows the correct way to go about it. Now, I wonder if the little Lady Leslie might be . . . ?

Parsons was more than ready to settle down in England and see an end to the duke's roving ways.

The Duke of Kenelm, strolling down the street in the attractive small town, was feeling pleased, for the young Endales' sake as well as his own, that he had spirited them away so quietly from Kenelm village. His peers might well look askance at the ploy, but Drogo had witnessed the white, frightened faces of the children, and heard the conviction in Leslie's voice when she told him that Wardell wished to murder his cousin.

It seemed possible to the duke that something unsavory might be going on. After all, someone—Wardell?—was buying up all the land adjacent to Endale. Why bother to add so heavily to his own administrative problems as guardian unless he intended profiting in the long run? No, taking the Endales to their elderly aunt in London was a sensible move, the duke assured himself. And in concealing from Wardell and the villagers the clandestine departure, he had behaved, he felt, with admirable sensitivity and decorum. The redoubtable peeress to whom he was delivering the young Endales would no doubt applaud his concern.

A comfortable thought.

Returning to the inn refreshed, Drogo set himself to observe the children. They were well-bred, bright, and charming. Someone had made a good piece of work of training them; their easy, friendly manner was not acquired by chance. His thoughts ranged back to his own parents, whom he had hardly known and certainly disliked. He could not recall a single instance in which either his dissolute (and later, sanctimonious) papa or his languid, self-pitying mama had ever given so much as a single word or gesture of concern for their only child's behavior—so long as it did not disturb their selfish lives! Not for Drogo Trevelyan the loving encouragement he had observed being so lavishly bestowed upon the younger Endales by their quiet sister. Perhaps he should acquire *her* services to encourage and cosset *him*, the duke thought with a grim half smile—and was surprised to hear Leslie's clear little voice addressing him, on cue!

"Is something wrong, Your Grace? Can I help you?"

"You may begin by calling me Drogo," the man said crossly. "We are close enough for that, surely?" *And will be closer*, he vowed, his mind made up. He intended to possess the little female, not for her dazzling charm—non-existent!—but for her ability to soothe, encourage, and cosset those she cared for. In his male arrogance, it did not occur to Drogo to wonder if the quiet Leslie could care for him.

Chapter 13

Riding in his elegant carriage toward London two days later, the duke surveyed his little party complacently. The three girls were ranged demurely across from him on the rear-facing seat, leaving ample room for their brother to sit or curl up on the luxurious squabs beside the duke. The two younger girls, quite enchanted by the appearance and attentions of their noble host, were chatting quietly together about their approaching visit to London. Only Leslie, who looked, thought Drogo, completely charming in Parsons' purchases, seemed rather distrait.

The Endales paid for dressing, as Parsons would probably say, Drogo mused. Lord Daryl, restored to health with the rapid resilience of childhood, had gone up on his knees to peer out the window, and was bedeviling his sisters with questions about a strange-looking beast in a field they were passing. Hilary suggested it might be a unicorn, but Meredith, also leaning forward to peer, said that she discerned *two* horns.

"Would that make it a dragon or a chimera?" quizzed Daryl with a twinkle. Drogo was inclined to admire the little earl. He had had nothing to do with children, and did not believe he would ever wish to, but Daryl was proving himself to be an intelligent, bright, and manly little fellow, who never whined or made demands upon his Benefactor. He was clearly not *spoiled*, in spite of his sisters' obvious devotion—or perhaps because of it? A provocative thought for a man who had never known what it was to be petted and cosseted by a mother or a sister.

Drogo's fine golden eyes moved contemplatively across the three feminine countenances under the modish bonnets. A handsome family, he decided, in spite of the odd kick in their gallop. For of course, the duke could put only limited credence in their tall tale of a Gothic Guardian with murder on his mind.

Drogo told himself that by late that night he would be rid of the bothersome children at last: his duty done to a fellow nobleman. Let Lady Bella sort out the problem with the encroaching heir. She was most definitely capable of dealing with a man far more alarming than the land-hungry Wardell!

Having mentally sloughed off his ill-fitting responsibility, Drogo expected to feel a sense of release. He tried to bring up in memory a list of desirable females of his acquaintance, one of whom might be persuaded to amuse him for a few weeks, but in the middle of this usually entertaining review, he caught an inquiring glance from Leslie, and found himself as embarrassed as though he had introduced a risqué topic in front of the children.

Leslie, mistaking his sudden frown for annoyance at the girls' and Daryl's constant babble, made haste to apologize.

"It should not be long now, sir, before you are free of us. I must tell you again that we can never repay our debt to—" she chuckled naughtily "—our Benefactor."

"And what," countered Drogo, for some reason wishing to be unpleasant, "if old Lady Endale refuses to accept you?"

Leslie refused to rise to the bait. "Then we shall simply have to find a way to support ourselves until Daryl reaches his majority," she replied.

The duke glared at her. "Foolish child! You have no conception of the perils, the ugly realities which await you in the streets of London. Have you ever visited the town?"

Leslie was no longer smiling. "No," she admitted soberly.

"But you have met your great-aunt?" persisted the duke.

"No," whispered the girl.

Shocked, Drogo stared at her downcast countenance. "I

do not *believe* what I am hearing!'' he announced, in such an angry voice that all three younger children ceased their quiet prattle and stared at their host. He controlled himself with an effort, and went on more quietly, ''You have never met the woman? You have no idea, then, whether she will agree to accept you all into her home?'' With rising suspicion, he added, ''Why is it that you have never met your father's aunt?''

''She quarreled with her brother,'' admitted Leslie, ''and as a consequence, refused to speak to him, or my father, or even my mother. And of course, not to their children,'' she added miserably.

The duke exhaled noisily. ''*Now* you tell me!'' he thundered. ''After you have wheedled me into aiding you to run away from your legal guardian and your family home! Do you wish to have me hauled up before the magistrates on a charge of kidnapping?''

Meeting that blazing golden glare, Leslie herself caught fire. ''I told you two days ago I would rather take the stagecoach to London! Had you sensibly agreed to my suggestion then, there would now be no chance of your being *hauled up* anywhere! If you will give your coachman the office to stop at the next inn, I shall relieve you of our distasteful presence forever!''

Into the shocked silence that greeted this emotional outburst, Hilary's voice came with a wail. ''Oh, sister! How can you address our Benefactor so! After all he has done for us! These pretty redingotes! The darling bonnets! And the *shoes*, Leslie! I have never worn handsomer ones. But of course, if you insist upon our leaving the duke's protection, we shall have to give it all back,'' Hilary concluded with a desolate sniffle.

Oddly pleased by this hysterical oration, the duke waited with interest for Leslie's reply. When the girl had nothing to say, but merely sat, frowning unhappily, he prodded in self-righteous tones, ''Your sister has expressed her very sensible doubts of your ill-advised scheme. Of course you cannot arrive in the wickedest city in the world unescorted, and with no knowledge of how to find safe and suitable lodging! Let me hear no more of this dangerous nonsense. You are alarming your sisters and brother,'' he added gratuitously.

With a sinking heart, Leslie was forced to acknowledge that the duke was right. She had not planned well, snatching the children away from their home without first making sure that their great-aunt would receive them. And it was equally true that, if Lady Bella refused to accept them, Leslie had no idea where to go or what to do to provide for her siblings. The one thing she was sure of was that she would never let Daryl return to March Wardell's guardianship.

Into her sober meditation intruded the clear voice of Meredith. ''Is London really the wickedest city in the world, Drogo?'' she asked.

Opening her mouth to chide her sister for the unauthorized use of their Benefactor's name, Leslie met his mocking smile and held her peace.

When he was sure she did not intend to argue the matter, Drogo addressed the question.

''Well, perhaps Marseilles is worse, or Port Said. . . .'' He grinned. ''I have not made a thorough study of the matter.''

Afraid that Meredith, in her innocence, might demand details, Leslie hastened to change the subject. It disturbed her to see how completely her siblings had accepted Drogo Trevelyan into their family circle. Even more disturbing was the manner in which their reluctant host seemed to be accepting his role, not only as Benefactor, but lately as guardian, instructor, and could it be—*friend*? An alien warmth began to suffuse Leslie's body at the thought. She stared searchingly into the handsome countenance across from her. It was animated, a roguish smile teasing the lips as he joked with Hilary. *Danger!* advised Leslie's mind.

Fortunately—or unfortunately—Lady Bella was at home when the ducal carriage pulled up in front of her austere mansion in Cavendish Square. One groom hopped smartly down from the box and ran up to belabor the heavy brass knocker, while a second servant opened the carriage door and let down the steps. He assisted the weary girls and the little boy down to the pavement, and then glanced inside to see if his master intended to accompany the party to their destination.

Heaving an obvious sigh of resignation, which he made sure Leslie noticed, Drogo got out and stood towering above his small charges. With unexpected kindness, he smiled encouragingly at the tired, apprehensive faces raised so trustingly to his.

"Forward the troops," he rallied them cheerfully. "You must lead us in the assault, Endale!"

Grinning, the boy offered his younger sisters each an arm. "I am making sure I have enough support," he said with an excellent imitation of a military snap.

Everyone chuckled. The duke offered his arm to Leslie, and the shared joke carried them triumphantly through the moment of confrontation as the massive doors were flung open and a formidable butler glared down his nose at the oddly assorted crew.

Daryl took the offensive.

"I am Endale," he said clearly. "I have brought my sisters and a friend to call upon my great-aunt."

Bravo, Daryl! thought Leslie, glancing at the big man beside her to see what he thought of her brother. Although his face now bore the cool arrogance that was his wonted expression, he met her glance with admiration in his own eyes.

The butler, refusing to be disconcerted by the motley party, now transferred his cold glare to the most important figure.

"Your name, sir?" he dared to ask.

"I am Kenelm," said Drogo icily. "I shall explain my business here to Lady Bella—when I am permitted to see her." The words were clearly a threat, and the butler, recognizing the authentic voice of authority, bowed at once

65

and silently ushered the party into the spacious, cold, ill-lit hallway.

Drogo, every inch the duke, made a thorough survey of the premises—and then sniffed disparagingly.

Leslie, caught as much by surprise as the butler, was forced to throttle a laugh. Drogo's single action informed everyone who heard him exactly what he thought of the townhouse of Lady Bella.

Drogo added to the butler's rout by instructing the top-lofty servant, "You may announce us to your mistress in the following form of address: 'The Most Noble the Duke of Kenelm, The Right Honorable the Earl of Endale, Lady Leslie, Lady Hilary, and Lady Meredith Endale.' Do you have that?"

With deep chagrin, the butler paced across the echoing hallway to a large pair of doors, which he thrust open with as much éclat as he could manage, coughed, said "mi-lady," and then delivered the required announcement.

The young Endales were too busy enjoying the rout of the formidable butler to be nervous at meeting their great-aunt. They advanced into the cluttered drawing room with bright smiles on their faces, which slowly changed into surprise and then alarm as a towering female figure in pseudo-Grecian robes swept toward them aggressively.

"What is this I am supposed to welcome into my home?" demanded Lady Bella. "A gazetted rake, three nondescript females, and a small boy—"

"I am your great-nephew Daryl, Aunt Bella." The boy's voice rang clearly into the silence his four companions were too affronted to break. "My sister Leslie thought you might offer us sanctuary. My cousin Wardell wishes to kill me." A wide smile broke across the solemn little face lifted so confidently to the old woman's. "Of course, you may feel the same way after I have been here for a while, but I am sure you are too intelligent to try it. You are not my heir, after all."

Had he known her intimately for a dozen years, Daryl could not have found a better way to pique Lady Bella's interest. She was a lonely, rather bitter old woman whose only real satisfaction in a long life had been her ability to use a good mind in intellectual matters. She gloried in the title of bluestocking, and led her literary, artistic, and even scientific soirees with brilliance and verve. So it was that Daryl's comment was the one sure way to unlock her rigidly guarded emotions.

She scanned the small face turned up to hers for a long moment. And then, "Welcome, Endale," she said crisply. Next, she stared hard at the duke, who met her searching scrutiny with bland attention. "Humph," she said finally, "I know what to think of *you*, sirrah!"

When he grinned boyishly, her hard expression softened minutely. "Oh, you're a charmer, I give you that! But with such parents as you had to suffer, a lunatic and a whiner, it is a wonder you emerged with your sanity intact."

Without waiting to see the effects of this devastating comment, she turned finally to scrutinize the three girls. Her eyes rested longest upon Meredith, and then returned to Leslie.

"You are?"

"I am Leslie—" began the girl.

"Named, like your sisters, because my nephew had a consuming desire to create heirs," snapped Lady Bella. "Why did you not change your male names when your parents died?"

Leslie felt quite unable to defend her failure to take an action she had never even considered.

Meredith, however, was nodding comprehension. "I think, Aunt Bella, that by the time my parents were killed, we had grown to like our names. After all, Hilary means the Cheerful One; and Leslie means One Who Owns Property," the little girl giggled, "although she will probably have to marry to get it, since all ours is entailed on Daryl! And of course, Meredith means Protector of the Sea. Do you think I should join the navy?"

Almost against her will, Lady Bella found herself smiling back at the child. Obviously an intelligent urchin, and had done some reading! She looked with a kindlier eye upon her unexpected guests. Then, capitulating, she waved her hand toward the numerous padded chairs and sofas that filled the room.

"You might as well sit down," she said. "Since I am sure you are going to stay. Meredith, will you pull the bell for Weems? He is no doubt hovering just outside the door, listening to what we are saying."

The door opened before Meredith could touch the bell-rope. "Yes, milady?" asked Weems crossly.

"Refreshment for His Grace and for my great-nieces. I am sure you will know what to serve Lord Drogo, and Cook will be pleased to furbish up a dish of treats for the children. Bustle, man! I'll have a glass of brandy with the duke."

For the first time since he had entered the mansion, Drogo relaxed. It was going to work! Those amazing little Endales had done it again! He was only thankful that Hilary had not seen fit to flaunt her delicate emotions upon the old harridan in the toga. His gaze shifted to Leslie, now giving polite answers to a stream of questions from Lady Bella. She had reached an explanation of their reasons for seeking sanctuary in London: the vicious horse, the mysterious fire. Drogo waited with resignation for Lady Bella's rejection of the charges against Wardell.

He was agreeably surprised when the old harridan nodded.

"I know little of March Wardell, except that he married a rich cit's daughter of remarkable plainness. He has never sought me out, and a good thing, for I would have had Weems refuse him! I can quite accept that he might wish to dispose of the earl. As long as Wardell was content to stay in the country, he could lord it over the rustics, and his wife might even come to be received some day."

"But *murder*?" objected Drogo.

"To gain an earldom? Why not?" countered Lady Bella. "It is not an act unknown in English history. And you cannot tell me there was anyone left who cared a rap what happened to these children."

"It appears that you, ma'am, might learn to do so," said

Drogo quietly, just as Weems entered, leading two footmen bearing trays, to the immense delight and satisfaction of the Endales.

Chapter 14

Not unexpectedly, Leslie was summoned to Lady Bella's bedroom the following morning, and invited to share a cup of tea. For a sensible period the two women remained silent, assessing each other carefully.

The old woman saw a tall, too slender girl—not surprising in view of the desperate journey through the woods! A thick mane of shining dark hair framed a delicately featured face. One's first impression was of modesty and breeding, but little sparkle. *Until you see her eyes*, thought Lady Bella, fascinated by the large, slightly slanted, light blue eyes framed in thick dark lashes. They mirrored and reflected every change of emotion. The girl has *possibilities*, decided Lady Bella, and broke the measuring silence.

"You were too tired, and I was too surprised, to begin a real acquaintance last night," she said briskly. "I must admit that, had I been consulted before you arrived, I should have denied you the sanctuary your brother demanded. Oh, I am not withdrawing my support," she amended quickly, seeing the startled expression on Leslie's vulnerable face. "I am coming to believe that I shall find you Endales both a stimulus and a challenge. I may have been getting a little too narrowly set in my thinking," she decided.

Leslie was still wary. "I shall endeavor to find work as soon as possible, and relieve you of our presence," she began quietly. "Perhaps you might recommend me to one of your friends as a companion—or even a dresser?"

Lady Bella's response to the manifest absurdity of this request was a disparaging sniff. For some reason this reminded Leslie so sharply of Drogo's unspoken comment upon entering the mansion last night that she could not help laughing.

Lady Bella eyed Leslie's face with surprise. "You should laugh more often," she said briskly. "It quite transforms your face. Well, I had better get started. I see I have much to do," she mused.

"Much—?" Leslie's anxious face revealed her confusion.

"To bring you into fashion," her amazing relative informed her. "We can afford to wait to launch your sisters into the ton. Hilary is too young and too unstable to be fired off into what Lord Byron called 'A Feast of Vultures.' Of course, he was speaking about war when he wrote that," she explained kindly, "but make no mistake, the social battle for consequence is a *war*! I myself have never desired to enter the lists. As for Meredith, it seems to me that she is capable of more important things than captivating a group of pampered, self-satisfied males. She may never desire to make her debut into the beau monde. But you, my girl, have distinct social potential." She cocked her aged head to one side, evaluating the slender figure before her. "Yes, I believe you could be shaped into something quite special to titillate the jaded taste of the *ton*."

Leslie had had her mouth open to set this opinionated old woman to rights, but as the meaning of what she was saying began to penetrate her mind, a wild hope sprang up. *Could* Leslie Endale—tall, thin, plain—become something "quite special"? Special enough to interest one in particular of the "pampered, self-satisfied males"? It was too enticing a suggestion to be dismissed out of hand. She stared at her great-aunt warily.

"Exactly what could be achieved, ma'am—*had you but world enough, and time*—say *a thousand years* to train my eyebrows to a suitable arrogance, two thousand to mold the rest of me into a coy . . . charmer?" Leslie misquoted Andrew Marvell with a twinkle.

"Aha! The chit is a bluestocking!" cried the older woman with real delight. "Grand-niece, whence had you this knowledge of the metaphysical poet—and one of his naughty love poems at that?" quizzed Lady Bella.

"My dear mama often read to us, when she put us down to sleep," said Leslie. "She was as likely to choose a love poem as a nursery rhyme."

There was a little silence. Then Lady Bella drained her teacup and said gruffly, "I wish I had known her. I was foolish to permit a disagreement with my brother to cut off all communication with the rest of his family. Not that I regret quarreling with Thomas," she amended hastily. "But I fear I missed a great deal in ignoring your parents, my child."

"They were happy," said Leslie slowly. "Like two loving children! I often felt that I was their parent, rather than the reverse."

"You have done a praiseworthy job of raising the earl," admitted Lady Bella. "And Meredith has clearly been encouraged to develop her intelligence. Hilary is still a closed book to me, but I shall not mind her presence here, I think." She nodded firmly. "I believe I like you all."

Leslie had to smother a grin as she looked at the older woman. Lady Bella's attire this morning was no less striking than the Grecian chlamys or whatever it was she had worn last night. Upon her head she sported a turbanlike nightcap, which emphasized her long, horsey face. As a bedgown, she had donned something that more closely resembled a tent than anything else Leslie could think of. Out of it her old arms and hands thrust, wrinkled and age spotted, as she handled her delicate teacup and saucer with elegant ease. The most striking feature in the leathery old countenance was a pair of deep blue eyes, bright and alert now as she contemplated the girl.

"Yes, I am going to enjoy having you young Endales with me," she announced. "It will be a new kind of challenge. The first thing to do is buy you all some suitable costumes."

Leslie felt an unaccustomed warmth. "I think this is

very pretty," she protested, running her hand lightly down the front of the redingote the duke had purchased.

"Oh, Kendale had good taste—or his valet does," Lady Bella admitted, "but you are not going to tell me that one decent traveling costume will be enough for a London Season?"

"Are we to have a Season?" whispered Leslie, suddenly very frightened at the turn of events.

"*You* are," conceded her great-aunt. "The others are too young—thank God! I rather doubt even *my* ability to launch all four of you at once!"

And suddenly she laughed, and Leslie laughed, and everything was right, and safe, and rich with delightful promise.

The only flaw in the next exciting week was the complete absence of any word from the duke. For the first three days Leslie had been afraid he would call—and for the last four she had been afraid he would not. What was wrong? Was he ill? Had he gone back to his notorious haunts in Europe, to continue the dissolute life he had lived there? Or had he, perhaps, returned to Kenelm to get on with the restoration of his family estates which he had mentioned to her?

Leslie still felt a pang of guilt when she recalled that it was her stupid intervention, with her siblings and their problem, that had forced His Grace to cut short his plans. Of course he would have returned at once to undertake the monumental task of rebuilding! To her surprise, Leslie discovered that she would give a great deal to be at his side, helping with the restoration. Oh, learning to be a debutante was fun, and a challenge, but working with Drogo Trevelyan would have been . . . pure joy!

One evening, after a long and difficult day with the couturier, coiffeur, and dancing master, great-aunt and niece faced each other over a delicious dinner. The occasion was far from somber, since all three younger Endales had joined them at the board, and questions and comments flew like arrows amid much laughter. Wiping tears of mirth from her eyes at some barbed comment from Hilary, Lady Bella chuckled.

"It was the wisest move of a brilliant career when I brought you children here to London," she said.

Provocatively mimed expressions of disbelief sent the old lady off into another fit of laughter. "Oh, very well! When you ruffians forced your way into these chaste Halls of Athene, then!" She peered around at the four bright, laughing faces with affection. "Well, let's have a report! What have you done today, Endale?"

"Rode my new horse—he's a beauty, Aunt Bella! Plenty of spirit, but a sweet nature. And no, I didn't fall off! Then I studied my books." This last was said with such a change of tone that all the females giggled.

"Oho, Daryl," chided his great-aunt, laughing, "you show less enthusiasm for education than for equitation, that's plain! Don't forget you must manage your estates when you're older. Endale demands that Endale accomplish!"

The mention of his estates brought a sudden halt to the general merriment. Ever lurking, in Leslie's mind, at least, was the threat of March Wardell's legal guardianship. The girl turned to her great-aunt.

"Have your men-of-law been able to find a way to place us under your aegis, rather than Wardell's, ma'am?" she asked.

Lady Bella pursed her lips. "I have not heard from them yet, although I placed the matter in their hands the day after you arrived," she informed them. "It is not unusual for the process of law to be ponderous—and devilish slow." She frowned. "Still, I believe I had better make inquiries as to their progress."

Observing the faces gravely sobered by this mention of their frightening problem, the old woman hastened to change the subject. "And you, Hilary? How have you spent your day?"

The pretty little face lighted up with excitement. "I had a fitting for a new costume and the darlingest pair of boots! Thank you, Aunt Bella! And then I had a dancing lesson, with Meredith. We *love* the gavotte! Much livelier than the minuet! And then our maid washed and brushed my hair into different styles, so that we might decide which suits me best!'' She dimpled at them from under her crown of shining golden hair. ''Isn't it pretty? Bartel is a jewel!''

''I wish she could make me look as well,'' grumbled the old lady, but no one was deceived. Lady Bella had no desire to titivate. ''Burnish the mind, not the countenance,'' she had said to Hilary one morning when the girl was coaxing her to join the female Endales in a grooming session.

''And that's all you've been doing?'' demanded Lady Bella.

Under the incredulous glances of her siblings, Hilary blushed. ''I have been learning French with Mr. Randolph, the tutor you provided for us,'' she confessed softly, ''and he has me reading Shakespeare.'' The last word was a whisper.

Bella crowed with pleasure. ''French and drama! Thank God you are not the pin-brain I feared!''

Hilary put on an offended pout, while her siblings hooted.

The old lady turned to Meredith. ''And you, little one? How have you busied yourself while I struggled mightily to give Leslie a little town bronze?''

''I idled away most of the time in your library, ma'am,'' said Meredith solemnly. ''Nothing so earth-shaking.''

''Were you bored, child?'' demanded the old woman sharply.

Meredith chuckled. ''You know I was not—*could not be*. Weems had to rout me out in time to dress for dinner.''

Lady Bella's eyes sparkled with satisfaction. ''What were you browsing over?''

Meredith's laughing expression faded. She peered at her siblings warily. ''Uh . . . *Harvey's Lectures on the Whole of Anatomy* . . .''

Three pairs of startled eyes and one pair warmly admiring met her tentative gaze. No one spoke for a moment.

75

Then, "Science, eh?" mused her great-aunt. "Not quite the easiest course for a young lady to follow."

"*Me*-re-dith!" gasped Hilary. "That's *worse* than a bluestocking!"

"What shall we call her?" asked Daryl, grinning. "Since bluestocking doesn't fit the crime?"

"Lady Sawbones?" giggled Hilary.

"Miss Bandage?" suggested the earl.

Leslie smiled happily. What a blessing, she was thinking, that Lady Bella had taken the young Endales into her household, and under her protection. There was quite possibly no other set of circumstances that would have given them all an access to their heart's desire: Daryl, training necessary to discharge his family duties well; Hilary, a chance to develop her mind as well as her social graces; Meredith, the opportunity to exercise her fine intelligence in fields normally quite "unsuitable" for young females. And herself? What was her dream, her destiny?

Unbidden, unwelcome, an arrogant, beautiful male face and figure came into her mind. *No!* Foolish beyond permission to consider Drogo Trevelyan. Absurd to pin her hopes on a closer relationship with one whom her great-aunt had labeled, probably justly, a gazetted rake. Still, he had returned to England. He was planning to restore his damaged heritage. Surely this was not the work of a . . . rake?

Leslie set her chin at a defiant angle. Rake or not, she found him fascinating, and longed to see him again.

Lady Bella, who had been watching with deep interest the changing expressions that moved across Leslie's face, now said crisply, "Well, Leslie, what is *your* plan of action? To conquer the beau monde, of course! For the sake of the Endale consequence, you must have a success, and receive at least two good offers, and marry well! But beyond that?"

Leslie drew a deep breath. "I shall be satisfied with *one* good offer," she said quietly.

Strangely enough, the others forbore to question her.

Although he had sent flowers to all four ladies, and

handsome riding crop to the young earl, the duke had not appeared in Cavendish Square since that first night when he had delivered the Endales to their great-aunt. The younger ones had mentioned his absence, but Leslie had not tried to make excuses for his failure to pay a duty call. "He knows how well-suited we are with Aunt Bella," she had said with rather a strained smile.

Lady Bella, pursing her lips slightly, changed the subject. There was a great deal more to this tall, quiet girl than was revealed on the surface. One glance at the huge, beautiful eyes in that small, vulnerable face informed any knowledgeable person of Leslie's unexpected depths. It seemed clear to the old woman that her great-niece had a youthful infatuation for the arrogant, beautiful Drogo Trevelyan. Lady Bella, while she appreciated the dazzling fellow's charm and allure, had no intention of permitting any girl in her charge to fall so far under his spell as to do anything foolish.

Not that Lady Bella thought Drogo was deliberately trying to ensnare the chit. No, his behavior had been unexceptionable: He had delivered his unwanted charges promptly to the door of their duenna; he had sent elegant *cadeaux* to their hostess and them; he had correctly forborne to pursue the casual acquaintance.

Yet Leslie as not the usual young debutante, mused the old woman. Unexpectedly she chuckled. Perhaps Lord Drogo, that polished seducer, had met his match at last! Lady Bella set herself happily to await developments.

Chapter 15

Although Drogo Trevelyan's cronies would not have credited it had they heard the report, the duke was in truth thinking seriously of undertaking the restoration of his family's primary estate. Lawyer Muir, apprised of His Grace's intention, could not at first believe his ears. Then he was betrayed into almost maudlin admiration.

"My dear boy! What a splendid decision!" Then, catching sight of Drogo's quizzically raised eyebrow, the lawyer recollected himself, and continued dryly, "I *thought* I had understood you to say that Kenelm Place could fall into rack and ruin for all you cared?"

The duke had the grace to color slightly, but his gaze was steady as he explained, "I had rather an interesting experience when I was checking on the offer to buy Kenelm. Oh, by the way, you were right. It is almost certain that the Mysterious Purchaser is March Wardell, the young earl's guardian—who is," he interjected with a frown, "fairly well thought of among the county bigwigs."

Muir pursed his lips. "I take it you do not share the general admiration?"

"I have not met the fellow, but I have taken a dislike to him," admitted the duke. "But not without some evidence, I hasten to assure you! You see, the *interesting experience* of which I spoke was meeting, in my attics at Kenelm, with the little earl and his sisters." A reminiscent grin tugged at his lips. "An unusual family," he added. "Have you by any chance encountered them?"

Highly diverted, the lawyer shook his head and waited for the story.

"I had just been deposited at my front door—oh," Drogo interjected, "I've dismissed that lumbering oaf you had keeping the gates. Parsons hired me a substitute. You'll get the bill. As I say, I was standing in the front hallway when I heard . . . sounds coming from overhead. Of course, I thought it was thieves—gypsies, perhaps, come to pick at the carcass! So I armed myself with a candlestick and raced upstairs. To find—" and he grinned "—the Earl of Endale being sick in my father's bed, and his sisters rifling through my family's old clothes in the attics."

Before the fascinated eyes of his lawyer, the duke's grin became a laugh. "The two younger girls had resurrected an ancient bonnet each from the boxes, and were wearing them with absurd panache. The older girl, Leslie—" Drogo's smile reached his eyes, and he paused in his account. Then, shaking his head, he went on in a softer voice, "Lady Leslie was . . . er . . . bent over, delving into a huge old trunk. You see, they had been running away from March Wardell for several nights through drenching rain, hiding out under bushes or in hollow tree trunks by day. They were thoroughly soaked, cold, and very hungry—Although Leslie had pinched some brandy, and kept them alive with sips of that!"

The unaccustomed boyish grin was back on the duke's well-cut lips. Lawyer Muir regarded his most notable client with deep interest. Whatever had stirred the normally bored and arrogant nobleman to such amused appreciation was to be cherished, since it had plainly aroused his dormant interest in his ancestral estates.

"They were running away from March Wardell?" Gently the lawyer nudged at his client's obviously pleasant preoccupation.

Drogo frowned. "It came out that their guardian had arranged a couple of 'accidents' which might easily have proved fatal to the earl. Leslie was seeking sanctuary in my home—which, according to common gossip, was empty and abandoned. The Endales were in fairly desperate plight, as you may imagine, and were searching for dry, clean garments and, after that, some food to strengthen them for their final desperate dash to London to appeal to their father's aunt, Lady Bella Endale.''

"I have heard of that lady," murmured Lawyer Muir, smothering a grin.

"The militant bluestocking," nodded the duke. "We five broke the square and routed her, foot, horse, and verbal attack! Lord Daryl was self-possessed, and his sisters utterly charming. Lady Bella accepted the appeal, and they are now safe under her shield.''

"Well done!" agreed Muir, now eager to hear the rest of this provocative account. "You intend to sponsor them into the ton, then, do you sir?''

The duke stared at him as though he were mad. "Sponsor them? I hope never to set eyes on any of them again!''

Lawyer Muir had a sense of having somehow missed his step. "Never . . . ? But I thought I understood you to say . . .'' his voice trailed into silence as the duke glanced at him sharply.

"I intend going back to Kenelm and beginning a complete restoration," he said largely. "For some reason, this ridiculous invasion of my home has . . . has brushed away the cobwebs." Drogo shook his head slightly, as though not quite sure of what he was saying, and then grinned tauntingly. "I was sure you would greet my change of heart with cheers of encouragement, Muir. You've been going on at me for months about my obligations to the name and all that!''

Samuel Muir stared into the handsome, smiling face. He could see something new there, something he had had brief, vague glimpses of in a younger Drogo, but had thought long dead. A sense of boyish fun, of enjoyment—of *expectation*. Muir wondered what it was that had worked the change. Surely not a single visit to a home he had always claimed to hate? Could it be the defiant, charming young Endales who had stimulated his optimism?

Or perhaps one particular one of them?

Chapter 16

How the devil did I get into this squeeze? thought the duke morosely. He was astride his favorite stallion, Ajax, in the driveway before his stately home, watching the cheerful bustle of carpenters, stonemasons, and gardeners as they labored with goodwill to restore Kenelm Place. Even the architect he had brought down from London had been caught up in the general delight that the county's most important Great House was being rapidly returned to its former splendor. Drogo scarcely dared to show his face in Kenelm Village, so voluble was the pleased satisfaction of the locals, from peers to plebeians.

Yet, in the midst of the general euphoria that had been created by his decision, Drogo was aware that he alone failed to share it. He had a nagging sense of . . . failure? Discontent? Loss?

Annoyed, he cast a sharp eye over the scene, eager to discover something—*anything*—about which he could justifiably complain. There was nothing. Everywhere, from roofs to foundations, was cheerful bustle; dust flying; shouting and laughter and the racket of rebuilding. Everywhere men were intent upon their tasks and proud of the results of their labor. As he watched his servants, the duke felt a strange emotion rising in his breast, an almost feudal sense of responsibility, of *protectiveness*, of pride in his workmen busy at their tasks.

Immediately, of course, he denied the emotion. Was that man of the world, the sophisticated Duke of Kenelm, whose cold, impregnable heart was notorious throughout the beau monde, to admit to sentimental folly? The fault, he told himself rancorously, lay with a gaggle of urchins who had somehow managed to create within his well-hardened heart this greatly-to-be-deplored weakness. It was that ramshackle band of refugees who had breached his defenses, cut up his peace, leaving him open to the assaults of unfamiliar feelings.

Again, unbidden, there rose in his memory the sight of one small female with a quiet, guileless manner and wide, honest eyes. Had the little chit bewitched him? Damned if he could get her out of his head! With a heavy hand, he pulled the reins and set Ajax galloping down the long, winding driveway toward the gates. The horse was more than willing to enjoy a run, and Drogo told himself that it was the dust and commotion of the work on the mansion that had driven him away.

After half an hour's hard going, both man and horse were ready to return to the inn, which Drogo had in effect taken over as headquarters for himself and his staff. Parsons had quietly assumed command of the inn staff, to the relief of the Crosses. Everything was going so smoothly, Drogo told himself, that he had been lulled into a state of foolish vulnerability. And that was why the maddening image of Lady Leslie Endale haunted his days as well as his nights!

He would have to banish her image at once, the duke decided with a cynical curl to his lips. And the best way to banish one female, he had learned, was to substitute another, fresher charmer. Unfortunately, there were obstacles to this very sensible decision. For one thing, even had there been a variety of candidates available in the village—which there was not—Drogo discovered that he could not bring himself to indulge in lascivious play with the daughters or wives of his surprisingly loyal workmen. Not at all the thing, in spite of the wicked folktales concerning dissolute noblemen and farmer's daughters!

No, it suddenly became clear to the duke that he would have to take a run up to London to refresh himself with a little light dalliance in that sophisticated city. *You see,* he told the image of the serious little face that persisted in presenting itself to his inner vision, *I know the way to exorcise you!* So, much pleased with his own worldly *nous,* Drogo gave Parsons the word to pack.

Instead of the pleased relief the duke had expected from his valet, Parsons put on a Friday face.

"What's got into you?" Drogo demanded. "I should have thought you'd be capering for joy at a chance to escape this bucolic wasteland."

"We have our duties here, Your Grace," said Parsons stiffly. "I have discovered that one of the Cross sons, taught by his mama, shows astonishing skill as a cook. He prepared the excellent quenelles of veal you enjoyed last night. With a little help, he might come to equal Chef Jacques in our London townhouse. I am training him now to recognize the better wines. I have also found time to work with the new gatekeeper, a steady fellow who will not put up with nonsense, but who knows how to treat the gentry. And there is—"

The duke held up one arrogant hand. "Can I believe my ears? The urbane Parsons actually enjoying himself among the gape-seeds? Or have you discovered in yourself a secret desire to become a major-domo?"

The question had been mockingly asked. To Drogo's surprise, a dark tide rose in the valet's cheeks. *The imperturbable Parsons is actually embarrassed!* thought the duke. With a curious stare, he asked, "Would you care to become my butler at Kenelm Place, Parsons?"

After a startled pause, the valet said, with pride, "I should be honored to serve Kenelm in that capacity, Your Grace."

Ye gods! I am surrounded by feudal types who wish to become my liege men! I had better escape to London before they insist upon swearing fealty! thought the bemused duke.

Yet even while he mocked himself as well as the locals, Drogo still could not deny the small thrill of pleasure that his new status as liege lord gave him.

In the event, the duke left his newly appointed butler to oversee the alterations and repairs at Kenelm, and keep things running smoothly during his master's escape to London. The very real disappointment with which his departure was greeted by the whole population of the county kept a small, warm glow of emotion burning in Drogo's heart.

Parsons had given his master a list of things the valet believed to be essential to the smooth running of the refurbished mansion, things that could only be obtained in London. The architect, who flatteringly refused to return to the metropolis until his restoration of the noble house was completed to his satisfaction, had begged His Grace to choose certain furnishings to replace outworn or outmoded pieces.

"Your taste is impeccable, Your Grace. You will want to have the final decision, I am sure."

With earnest assurances from all the sundry that his affairs would be carefully dealt with in his absence, Drogo had set out on a journey he had originally planned as a casual, licentious fling, but that now had assumed both the dignity and the obligations of a ducal progress. And now, to cap his discontent, he discovered that he was affronted by the oppressive stench and haze of London.

Getting down from his carriage in front of his massive town house, Drogo wondered if the city had always smelled so stale and appeared so unappealing? *I am spoiled by bucolic freshness*, he mused wryly, striding through double doors held open by bowing footmen. Within an hour he was washed, changed, and ready to visit the clubs to pick up the latest *on dits* and hear of the reigning diamonds and charmers.

Six hours later he was again entering his house, oddly disappointed and disgruntled. He had found that most of his special cronies were either absent, drunk, or boring. The names of acknowledged beauties who were currently uncommitted to their noble husbands roused in Drogo none of the hunting instinct he expected, while the list of the available fashionable demimondaines struck him as remarkably unexciting. *What is the matter with me?* he wondered as he allowed himself to be prepared for bed by an inept substitute for Parsons. *I am already bored after only a few hours in the wickedest city in the world—well, one of the three wickedest,* he amended with a grin, remembering a conversation with the children during the drive to London.

Strangely, the memory of the Endales brought him a sense of pleasant expectation that he could not understand. Of course, he would not dream of calling in Cavendish Square to see how the brats went on! Quite the last thing he would ever wish to do, he assured himself. But what if old Lady Bella, driven mad by their juvenile excesses, had already gotten rid of the wretched waifs!

At the thought that the Endales might have disappeared, Drogo was forced to admit two things. First, that he had found the young Endales not only well-behaved but also delightful and fascinating companions. Second, that the Duke of Kenelm would be paying them a courtesy visit the very next morning, as early as custom permitted! In fact, decided the duke, the little Leslie had *better* be where he had so properly bestowed her, and not traipsing irresponsibly around an admittedly wicked city!

Quite unruffled by his surprising about-face, Drogo settled in happily for a good night's sleep.

The following morning, His Grace dropped into White's for a cup of coffee and the latest gossip before paying his duty call on Lady Bella. He hoped to discover whether anyone in the beau monde had become aware of the presence in London of the young Earl of Endale and his sisters, especially the eldest of them.

He was unpleasantly surprised.

It appeared that Lady Bella had indeed exerted herself to bring Leslie into the notice of the ton—with less than happy results. The youngest son of the Marquis of Tatom, whom Drogo had never considered worthy of more than a cool glance in passing, barged in brashly on a discussion that Drogo was conducting with an old school friend, Kevin O'Dare.

"If you're speaking of Lady Leslie Endale, I have a word of warning for you," said the complacent young buck. "I was dragooned by my mama—a bosom bow of the old bluestocking's—into dancing with the girl last night at mama's ball. The chit has no looks, no conversation, and she can't dance!"

"Then it is fortunate for *impecunious younger sons* that she has the wealth of a nabob, is it not?" asked Drogo with a sarcasm so cutting that it surprised even himself.

Kevin looked after the routed busybody with a grin. "I should say you put him pretty sharply in his place, old boy," he commented. "What's the Endale girl to you, Drogo? She's not precisely your style, surely?"

"You have met her?" Drogo demanded. "You were at the Tatom's last night?"

"For my sins," intoned Kevin with mock anguish. "A very boring evening, the food scanty and the liquor almost undrinkable. Fruit cup, or some such," he concluded with a shiver.

"Lady Leslie," prompted Drogo, bringing him back to the subject.

Kevin pursed his lips. "Well, she isn't the disaster young Lackwit suggested. She's very quiet, though, and so badly rigged out that she could be Venus and no one would realize it."

I knew it! groaned Drogo silently. *I should never have left her with that totty-headed old woman!* Aloud he said grimly, "She made a show of herself?"

Kevin shook his head. "No, I told you she was very *quiet*. Not at all the sparkling debutante who is constantly surrounded by adoring males." He frowned. It appeared his friend was in some way entangled with the little creature, and might be involved in her rejection by the ton. "I've never seen a worse getup, Drogo. If you have an interest in the chit, take her to the best dressmaker in London before she ventures into society again! She looked like the ingenue in a badly staged Italian farce. Of course, if she is as rich as Croesus, only the highest sticklers will

86

hold her appearance against her. An earl's sister, too," he finished supportively.

While Kevin was speaking, his expression had been growing more cheerful. He ventured a question. "What's the girl to you, Drogo?"

What, indeed? Drogo asked himself. Elevating his eyebrow dauntingly, he resurrected the earlier fiction. "I have an obligation to her father, a longtime neighbor of my family. The parents were killed in an accident a few months ago, and I had the . . . duty of bringing the orphans to their great-aunt. I had hoped," he finished grimly, "that Lady Bella would launch the girl successfully."

Kevin grinned. "You have been abroad, haven't you? Still, you cannot convince me that a man of your nous spent several years in London without at least hearing of old bluestocking! Had you actually imagined that bookish eccentric would know how to fire off a debutante?"

"I seem to have overestimated her flair," muttered the duke. "Well, I'll have to set things to rights."

Kevin's eyes widened. Could this elegant roué, this terror of matchmaking mamas, be planning to launch a plain little country bumpkin into the vicious arena that was the ton?

"May I help you, Drogo?" he murmured discretely. Then, at the sudden arrogant frown on his friend's face, he said quickly, "I know every hostess in London, and I'm in better odor with most of them than you are, you rakehell! Between us, we could get young Lady Leslie an invitation to almost any festivity in town. To say nothing of the fact that you are on good terms with the leading dressmakers in the town—having paid the bills for a dozen *belles amies* in your time."

Drogo regarded him sourly. "I suppose *you* have wheedled your way into the good graces of every hostess in the ton, but I don't trust you, you Irish rebel!"

Then, noting how Kevin immediately focused on the word *trust*, Drogo was quick to utter a disclaimer. "Oh, no, I've no personal interest in the chit, believe me! You have seen her. Can you imagine that *I* . . . ?" He cocked

87

a derisive eyebrow at his friend. "You know me better than that."

Kevin was reluctant to accept that the dissolute duke was ready to sponsor a little dab of a female into the beau monde for purely altruistic reasons, but surely there could be no sexual attraction. Kevin saw he would have to bide his time to discover the truth. Taking his friend's arm, he moved toward the doorway.

"Shall we call upon Lady Bella and her house-guests?"he suggested. "We can pick up bouquets on our way."

"Don't try your tricks on me, you Irish bog-trotter," warned Drogo, but the offer of such wily and knowledge-able assistance as Kevin could supply was too valuable to refuse. The two young bucks strolled out of White's arm in arm, arguing companionably over the proper *bijou* that would be acceptable to an elderly bluestocking.

Young Tatom, sulking in a corner, glared after them. It was strictly unfair that any one human being should have as much as Drogo Trevelyan: independence, wealth, viril-ity, golden good looks—and devastating charm, when he bothered to flaunt it!

As Drogo's carriage pulled up before Endale House in Cavendish Square, the duke idly noted a very drab-looking closed coach of ancient style waiting farther down the street, and wondered how any tradesman would have the brass to deliver his merchandise to the front door of one of these elegant mansions. It would have been better if he had glanced more closely at the solitary inhabitant of the ve-hicle.

Chapter 17

The descent of two elegant men-about-town upon the aged and irascible eccentric developed, not surprisingly, into an unpleasant confrontation. For one thing, Lady Bella was having second thoughts as to the wisdom of trying to force her great-niece upon the ton. The old bluestocking was no fool. She had enough nous to realize that, far from winning the admiration of the beau monde and a suitable offer or two, Leslie might all too easily become a humorous *on dit*, exposing both herself and her sponsor to the vicious sarcasm that passed for wit in high circles.

She was also a little concerned for Leslie herself. The girl was by nature quiet, but as the two weeks of preparation for the launching crept on, the chit grew pale, subdued, and obviously far from happy. Lady Bella, already apprehensive at the idea of failing in her sortie into a world she had always scorned, began to vent her fears upon the one she now described as the cause of them. In fact, she had just been haranguing Leslie on her spineless attitude toward her critics when Weems announced the Duke of Kenelm and Mr. Kevin O'Dare.

The gentlemen entered a room charged with tension. One glance at the red, angry face of Lady Bella and the pale, guilt-stricken countenance of the young girl informed both worldly-wise men that they had chosen an awkward moment to pay a courtesy call. Kevin, never at a loss socially, moved forward to play off his blarney on his elderly hostess. Drogo, quickly evaluating the situation, went to bow over Leslie's hand.

He was already aware that Leslie's first entrance into the ton had been a disaster: young Tatom had made that clear! As he knowledgeably scanned the too-mature, badly fitting, and hopelessly dowdy garment the girl sported as a morning gown, his heart sank. He should have realized that an elderly eccentric, who had very publicly scorned society for donkey's years, would be the last person to present a country innocent to a hostile group.

But what else could he have done? he asked himself, murmuring gracious nothings in a practiced way to Leslie as he worked through the problem. Putting aside the ignoble wish that he had never encountered the urchins in his attic in the first place, the duke began to organize his forces. First in order of importance must be to win Lady Bella over and convince her to follow his lead.

With this worthy end in view, Drogo gave a final, reassuring smile at the pale face turned with unconscious appeal up to his, and strolled forward to relieve Kevin.

Taking the old woman's hand firmly in his, he bent to touch his lips to the wrinkled skin, and then said, with his most seductive smile, "How delightful it is to see you again, Lady Bella!"

The old harridan was not about to let him off lightly. "We've seen nothing of you for two weeks," she snapped. "Leslie was sure you had gone back to your ruined estates at Kenelm. Not before time, I hear." She sniffed disparagingly.

So the girl had been talking about him, had she? For some reason, the thought was pleasant. Drogo gave her his most provocative smile, noted her blushing response with interest, and then addressed himself to the old woman again.

"I must admit that the demands of restoring Kenelm have been heavy, but naturally I could not forget my obligation to Endale. I have, in fact, with the help of my friend O'Dare, been mapping out a campaign for our little debutante," he said ingratiatingly. "Of course, we men do not wish to intrude, or force our callow ideas upon so notable an intelligence as your own, ma'am! But you must admit that between us, Kevin and I have considerable experience in . . . ah . . . *manipulation*—'' he cocked a wicked eyebrow ''—which we gained during our misspent youth. We dare to hope you will permit us to place it at your service on this occasion. And do not tell me, dear Lady Bella, that you would not enjoy diddling the dupes in the ton!''

While Kevin, endeavoring to conceal his surprise at this barefaced flimflam, silently paid tribute to a master manipulator, Lady Bella's grim resentment was beginning to fade into pleased, if still slightly suspicious, acceptance.

''Why should two such gazetted rakes as you and your friend O'Dare desire to help me?'' she demanded. ''Or has one of you an eye on the girl?''

This was plain speaking indeed, thought Drogo, saluting a worthy antagonist. He put on his blandest air of reproach, and said gently, ''The sister of the Earl of Endale? So very *youthful*, albeit charming, a bud? You wrong us, Lady B!''

The old woman joined in a laugh with Kevin and Drogo, but the latter noted that Leslie was not amused. *Oh, well, I'll handle her later,* he promised himself, and continued his skillful effort to dominate the elderly peeress.

In this he was brilliantly successful. Within half an hour, he had enmeshed the fascinated Lady Bella completely in his schemes, along with an eager Kevin, who foresaw just the hilarious sort of game he enjoyed playing. With the exception of an unusually sober Leslie, the members of the group enjoyed a delightful session, and all arrangements were made for a successful debut, including some that had Leslie's eyes widening, and quite shocked the sober Weems, eavesdropping in the hall.

Drogo managed to murmur a few words aside to Leslie while Kevin was making his skilled adieux to Lady Bella. ''I shall be talking with you in private tomorrow, when I call to take you for a spin through the park,'' he advised her.

"Will my great-aunt accompany us?" asked the girl woodenly.

"We shall be alone. It is quite *convenable*," he continued. "All fashionable London will be our chaperone."

"Why are you doing this . . . going to all this trouble for a youthful nuisance?"

Drogo was a little surprised at the bitterness in the quiet voice. The pretty ladies with whom he usually amused himself had scarcely shown so much feeling—under so firm a control—except perhaps in matters of a desired piece of jewelry or a new carriage. His eyebrows lifted in that habitual gesture Leslie both loved and hated.

"I have plans for you," he said quellingly.

Leslie gritted her splendid white teeth.

The duke caught the slight gesture and grinned unforgivably. "You did seek sanctuary under my shield," he taunted. "And now you must pay your debts." He laughed at the mingling of frustration, anger, and curiosity in her expressive little face. "No, you must wait until tomorrow to learn of my . . . special plans for you! And to receive my orders."

With a final rakish grin, he bowed and followed Kevin out of the mansion.

The sight of the dowdy closed carriage registered on his mind, but beyond a brief thought that it was oddly out of place in these elegant surroundings, he did not consider it further.

Chapter 18

Driving his smart curricle into Cavendish Square the following afternoon, Drogo flashed past the same black coach he had noticed the previous day. Something about it disturbed him. He pulled his horses expertly to a halt, backed the curricle to a position beside the dowdy vehicle, and bent down to peer into the small glass window.

A heavyset, plain-looking woman stared back at him.

The duke might have challenged a man. He found himself unable to ask this drab female what she was doing haunting the Square. After a moment, filled with annoyance, he gave his horses the office to proceed, and drew up shortly in front of Lady Bella's residence.

A footman was waiting to take the reins. With a word of caution concerning the spirited team, the duke strode up the stairs and through the front door Weems was holding wide for him.

"Lady Leslie is in the drawing room, Your Grace," the butler advised him. "I am afraid the children wish to greet you, also."

"Delighted," Drogo replied, and found that he meant it.

The young Endales gave him an enthusiastic welcome. Daryl shook his hand with a good firm grip, the blue eyes that were so like Leslie's meeting Drogo's warmly.

"Good to see you again, sir," Daryl said cheerfully. "Have you met any dragons or chimeras lately?" He grinned.

Drogo chuckled. "I fear we are sadly lacking in fabulous beasts here in London, Endale. But perchance we shall see a few unicorns in the park—now that Lady Leslie is in residence."

Leslie blushed; Hilary and Daryl looked blank. Meredith twinkled up at the teasing nobleman.

"Legend has it," she instructed her young siblings, "that unicorns will come to a virgin. The unicorn lays his head in the girl's lap. She strokes him, and holds him captive until the hunters come to catch him."

Hilary gasped in outrage. "What a cruel betrayal! When the poor creature was so trusting! I cannot credit that any female would be so false!"

"Credit it," advised Drogo cynically, as one who spoke from a wealth of experience. His mocking eyes sought and challenged Leslie's quiet gaze. She was not smiling. Her clear wide eyes seemed to be searching his face, the man thought, offering reassurance. . . .

Reassurance! Drogo caught himself up sharply. It was not possible that the Duke of Kenelm needed reassurance from some green girl without a scrap of town bronze! He hardened his heart.

"Why else do the delicate virgins flock to town, if it is not to snare some helpless male?"

"But that is surely not the same," protested Hilary. "The debutantes come to meet a suitable *parti*—or so Miss Wheaton advised us. It is a custom . . ." She hesitated, catching the taunting smile on Drogo's well-cut lips.

"The poor wretched males may run if they wish," Meredith pointed out. "They are not tied down!"

"Neither was the unicorn," Drogo reminded her. "The wily virgin puts him under a spell. It is *black magic*!"

He sent Leslie a mocking smile, inviting her response. Yet again the girl surprised him.

"I would never so betray one who trusted me," she said quietly. "Man or beast."

Drogo elevated his brows in ironic challenge, but the girl refused to comment further. With a sense almost of having lost a skirmish, Drogo informed the younger children that he would come to take them to a balloon ascension on the heath the following morning, and that they must be ready by nine o'clock sharp if they were to secure good positions to watch the spectacle. Then, followed by their expressions of gratitude and delight, he swept Leslie from the room, scarcely permitting her time to don her bonnet and shawl before pulling her down to the curricle.

As they drove away, he glanced curiously around the square. There was no sign of the black coach. He turned his attention to the girl seated so quietly beside him. Taking his time, he surveyed her costume.

"I shall have to get you to a decent couturier," he murmured. "I have written out a list of instructions for you, which you will follow to the letter." Catching a hint of rebellious anger in her carefully averted face, he went on smugly, "Some of the time I shall accompany you—for instance, when I am selecting your wardrobe. I shall choose for you an accomplished dresser, one who is up to all the fashionable rigs, and who has a sixth sense for the *avant-garde*. It will not be enough that you show alamodality," he continued, with what Leslie read as insufferable conceit. "I shall expect you to *lead* the pack, not follow it. *My protégée* must not do otherwise."

This last suave little taunt had the girl turning on the seat beside him, her expressive eyes blazing with anger.

"I beg to remind you, *Your Grace*, that I am not your 'protégée,' and in fact, from what I have picked up since I entered this wretched beau monde, I would be better without you as my sponsor! You are widely known to be a rakehell and a roué and—"

"Silence!" snapped the duke, with unforgivable hauteur. "If I say you are to do something, you will do it—with good grace!" His arrogant scowl lightened as he caught her furious glare of outrage at his high-handedness. "Not so much fun to be under my shield as you had envisioned?" he taunted softly. Then: "We are approaching the park. Smile gently if we are accosted by any of the fashionable fribbles. Unless I draw up the curricle to introduce some worthy *parti*, you will keep a distant, mysteri-

95

ous half smile upon your face. Acknowledge introductions with a mere, sighing 'How do you do?' which you will utter as though you did not care in the least. *That* will set them all to wondering, and pique their appetites.''

Leslie glared up into the arrogant, smiling face. ''Are you coaching me to become some fribble's light-o'-love? I am sure that is not what Great-aunt Bella is expecting!''

''I am relieving your elderly relative of an almost insupportable burden,'' her cruel mentor advised her. ''How can she, who is herself a mere babe-in-arms in the ton, fire off a little country nobody without a trace of nous, a green girl who lacks either presence or beauty. . . .'' The big man paused, startled at the look of desolation that swept across Leslie's vulnerable countenance. For the first time in a misspent, slavishly courted, too-pampered life, the Duke of Kenelm became aware of the pain one of his careless remarks had inflicted. Frowning, he wondered whether he should try to soothe the hurt. Then, scanning the now closed, small face, Drogo decided to let it go. It would probably make the chit more malleable if she had to face exactly how inept and unsuitable she really was for the course she and her great-aunt had chosen.

The ride into and through the park continued, with the duke being hailed upon all sides with flattering interest and, Leslie decided, considerable envy. She watched, her expression schooled as closely as possible to the required mysterious half smile, her response a correct, sighed 'How do you do?' at each presentation of a new buck or beau.

After half an hour of this, Leslie turned to Drogo and under cover of a bland smile, hissed angrily, ''How long is this farce to continue? You have not introduced me to a single female! Have you no women friends?''

Drogo's wicked grin gave her her answer, but the rogue said blandly, ''The hostesses your aunt and I hope may accept you do not spend their afternoons dawdling about Rotten Row.''

''Then why are *we* doing so?'' snapped the girl. ''I am sure that most of the silly clowns you have presented to

96

me today would not in any way bolster my chances of succeeding in the ton!''

''On the contrary,'' Drogo corrected her smoothly, ''when these silly clowns see you with the Duke of Kenelm, they will hasten to claim acquaintance with you at the next ball or soiree you attend . . . if only to try to discover what so notable and discriminating a rake saw in you,'' he ended.

Leslie set her jaw against a bitter retort. She must suffer any pain, dare any circumstance, to keep Daryl safe in London. Bowing her head with a meekness she was far from feeling, she refused to answer to Drogo's taunt.

The man watched her closely, hoping for a flare of rebellion. Then, realizing that she would not be drawn, he shrugged and drove out of the park and back toward Cavendish Place.

''I think that has been enough for your first lesson,'' he said mockingly. ''Before I present you to the ton again, I shall be sure your costume will not embarrass me. I shall pick you up tomorrow about noon for our first sortie into the world of *haute couture*.''

At this, Leslie's glance flashed up to meet his. ''You told the children—'' she faltered. ''The balloon ascension? They will be so disappointed!'' Her wide blue eyes pleaded for the young Endales' pleasure as they had never done for her own.

Almost gruffly Drogo admitted, ''I had indeed forgotten. But of course we shall attend the celebration. Try to wear a less hideous bonnet, if you have one.''

No other word was spoken until they reached Lady Bella's mansion. Drogo assisted Leslie down and escorted her to the door, which was swung open at their approach by the attentive Weems. With merely a brief nod and a stiff bow, Drogo turned away and ran lightly down to remount his curricle.

Weems and Leslie watched him drive off with regret and a deep sense of disappointment.

''He is bored with me, Weems,'' Leslie confided.

The old butler frowned. After a moment he advised, ''I

should not give up hope too soon, milady. These men-about-town are as notional and skitty as thoroughbreds. Completely spoiled by the ladies, they are, and as wary as foxes. You'll have your work cut out taming *that* one, Miss, if I say so as shouldn't!''

Leslie found herself unable to disagree with this grim prognostication.

Chapter 19

To everyone's surprise, several large and elegant boxes arrived in Cavendish Square for Lady Leslie Endale the following morning. These were brought up by Weems himself, who lingered near the door while Leslie and her aunt, who had risen early to consider the matter of bonnets, proceeded to open the boxes.

From the first, Leslie pulled out a ravishingly feminine pink bonnet, which had a pert garnish of silk wild roses. Everyone present admired the delicate little creation, but Lady Bella said doubtfully, "It's rather too plain, don't you think?"

Leslie (and Weems, sotto voce) hastened to assure her that indeed, it was not! Leslie sighed, "It does not *frighten* me as the other bonnets did, Aunt Bella. They are the *dernier cri*, I am well aware, but they are so . . . so *overpowering*, ma'am!"

Lady Bella was not sure whether or not to be offended by this description of her expensive, if unattractive, purchases. She resolved the problem by placing the new pink bonnet carefully on Leslie's head and then stepping back to view the result. Leslie held her breath, her eyes fixed on her great-aunt's stern countenance.

"Beautiful," decided the elderly dame, with a short nod.

"Very suitable!" agreed Weems. When both pairs of eyes swiveled toward him, he colored, bowed, and slid out of the room.

Lady Bella smiled. "That's the first time I've been able

99

to catch Weems off guard since he came to work for me," she said happily. "Let's see what's inside the rest of these boxes. I did not realize you and the duke had gone shopping yesterday."

"We had not," answered Leslie, looking stunned. "Do you suppose these are from *him*? How could he know . . . ?"

"You ask me that about Drogo Trevelyan?" chuckled her aunt. "The man's notorious for decking out half the light-skirts in the ton! He probably knows more—*oooh!*" The interjection was almost pushed from her as Leslie displayed the soft blue redingote trimmed with pink velvet to match the bonnet. "Is it . . . your size, child?" breathed the older woman.

"It must be!" half groaned the girl. It was unthinkable that this darling dress might be too small, or too large, or too anything but exactly right for her. Leslie immediately began to shed her clothing so that she might don the attractive garment; for once, Lady Bella made no effort to check the girl's impulsive actions.

In a few minutes the dress was on, and Leslie ran to the mirror and adjusted the pink bonnet. Then she turned delightedly to face her great-aunt.

"How do I look?" she demanded softly.

"Delightful," said Lady Bella, with complete honesty. "The man must be a black magician."

Leslie's smile faded just a little. "Are you sure it was the duke who sent these things?" she whispered.

"Who else?" shrugged Lady Bella. Peering keenly into the girl's face, she added wisely, "Be grateful, girl! You have been fortunate enough to enlist—God knows how!— the aid of an adviser of superior skill. Let us be thankful for it. And *quiet* about it!" She added a warning. "People might misunderstand."

Leslie's gaze had returned to the mirror. "How could he have known?" she wondered softly. "The redingote fits me as though it had been made for me. . ." She gave a worried frown.

The elderly peeress snapped her fingers briskly. "Open

the rest of the boxes, child," she instructed. "I cannot wait to see what else Trevelyan has chosen for you."

The contents of the other boxes produced sighs and cries of satisfaction. One box held a pair of blue kid boots which, though a trifle large, were still most suitable with the redingote. A silver-papered carton revealed some silk and lace undergarments which had Leslie blushing and Lady Bella giggling. The last box held a darling reticule which shimmered softly with tiny pearl beads. When, entranced, Leslie opened it, she found a lace handkerchief as delicate as cobwebs tucked inside, and a tiny vial of attar of roses.

Lady Bella drew a deep breath and peered over at the silent girl. "You will thank His Grace for his great kindness," she instructed.

Then, observing the dazzled delight on Leslie's face, she added sternly, "But not too warmly!"

Leslie giggled. Drogo's gift had sent her spirits rising. Surely no man who was coldly indifferent to a woman could have chosen that delightful little bonnet for her!

Firmly recalling her from her maidenly transports, Lady Bella set her to preparing herself for the excursion to the heath.

"The children . . ." murmured Leslie, slipping out of the new dress long enough to don some of the lacy undergarments.

"I shall see to them," promised Lady Bella largely. "But you—" She frowned. "Are you sure you can get yourself into those things?"

In the event, such inadequate self-help was proven unnecessary. A discreet tap upon Leslie's bedroom door produced a greatly impressed Weems who presented a tall, grim-faced female in somber black.

"I am Lady Leslie's dresser," announced this formidable female. Removing her bonnet and placing it, with a small case, unobtrusively on a small chair, she strode over to the startled girl and surveyed her carefully.

A painful silence ensued.

Lady Bella was too startled to speak, and Leslie too agonized by the searching scrutiny.

At length the woman nodded. "I think I can cope. The features are undistinguished, but the skin is flawless, and the eyes are remarkable. Hair I can do something with, I believe." She nodded again. "Lady Leslie, I am Cameron."

Lady Bella could not endure being overlooked for another instant.

"I am Lady Bella Endale," she intoned. "Your mistress's great-aunt."

"Yes, milady," said Cameron with icy primness. Would anything ever soften that critical regard? Leslie wondered.

"I am glad you have joined the staff," Lady Bella was saying repressively. "Weems shall provide you with a room and explain the rules of my establishment."

To Leslie's relief, Cameron did not take umbrage at this decisive set-down. She merely gave her curt nod and turned her attention once more to the slender girl.

"Allow me to adjust your redingote, milady," she commanded.

With a soundless *hmph!* the elderly bluestocking swept from the room. Providentially, Weems was holding the door open for her. In the hallway, he regarded his fuming mistress respectfully.

"It will do very well, milady," he said softly. "I recognize her sort. She is brusque, but she will devote her no doubt superior skills to . . ."

"To presenting little Leslie *en grand tenue*," snapped Lady Bella. "That reprehensible devil Trevelyan! He is turning our lives about to suit his casual whim! A dresser for Leslie, forsooth! And *such* a dresser!"

She set her lips against further indiscreet conversation with her old retainer, and went abruptly back to her own sitting room, determined not to acknowledge Drogo Trevelyan when he arrived to collect the children for the balloon ascension.

The treat was all Leslie might have hoped, and more. Her siblings were enthralled by the preparations for the balloon ascent. Meredith asked some remarkably astute questions, quite impressing the duke. Hilary enjoyed her usual dramatic posturing, so that Leslie was compelled to restrain her wilder flights. Wearing her new outfit, Leslie felt competent to handle even greater challenges than an excited child could present. She was constantly aware of the duke, suave and devastatingly handsome in his tight buckskins and modish coat. His wide white smile flashed, the upper lip thin, the lower full and sensuous. His eyes, making a leisurely survey of her from the top of the new bonnet to the tips of the blue shoes, glinted their approval of Leslie's appearance, but he said nothing about it. In fact, he addressed most of his comments to Daryl, with whom he carried on a pleasant conversation.

He is waiting for me to thank him for the clothes, thought Leslie. And of course I must do so, no matter how embarrassing I find it to acknowledge his generosity—and his knowledge of women's intimate apparel! She sent another sideways glance at the duke from under her eyelashes, which, to her delight, Cameron had subtly darkened with some magic process of her own.

She felt a shock of—*something*—as her seeking glance was met and challenged by a bold, mocking smile from her Benefactor. How can he manage to look so *charmingly wicked* without uttering a single questionable remark? She quickly lowered her eyelids lest he become aware of her infatuation.

His Grace was not so easily put off when he was on the hunt, she found. He moved over beside her as the attendants released the guy ropes and the gaily colored globe soared upward into the sky. The younger Endales were caught in awe and delight, and had no eyes for anything but the soaring balloon. Drogo took her arm in his big, hard hand.

Warmth spread through Leslie's body in a delicious surge. She raised her open, vulnerable glance to meet his predatory smile.

For a brief moment Drogo smiled down at her. Then his expression changed, hardened. He gripped her elbow so hard as to hurt a little, and then dropped his hand as though he, and not she, was feeling the warm torment.

Leslie stared up at him apprehensively. *What had she done to bring that cold, closed look to his face?*

"Your Grace—" she began.

"You will call me Drogo," he instructed sharply. "I grow tired of your girlish affectations."

This was like a dash of cold water. Leslie felt a comforting anger surge up within her, giving her courage to lash back at this arrogant male.

"I shall call you whatever I wish," she announced in a voice loud enough to attract attention from members of the throng close to them.

Drogo's eyebrows lifted in the irritating manner he affected. Then slowly a smile of genuine amusement softened the well-cut lips. "So!" he said softly. "the little cat has claws?" The warm hand returned to her arm.

"I am not," announced Leslie, carried away by hubris, "a cat, *Your Grace*. But you will find I have weapons of my own, unless you walk softly."

Drogo's shout of delighted laughter turned many heads in their direction, curious to discover the source of such unrestrained merriment. Leslie felt a wave of dismay, not only at attracting public notice, but also at her reckless folly in throwing down a gauntlet to so wily and powerful an antagonist.

Drogo pulled her close, making her very conscious of his hard, warm body. Smiling, he bent to murmur in her ear, "A declaration of war, Madame? I think I shall enjoy that!"

Her lips open to beg his pardon—for in truth he had already done more than anyone could expect for the runaway Endales—Leslie straightened her back and substituted a question for the apology she had been going go offer.

"It was you who sent me the dragon-dresser, was it not?"

"She is formidable," agreed the duke with a grin. "She will whip you into shape, little vixen."

"I wonder how you knew of such a one," said Leslie

104

airily. "Perhaps you have made use of her services . . . yourself?"

To this piece of outrageous libel Drogo made no direct reply. Instead he bent with a feral smile and kissed Leslie very hard on the mouth. Worse, he held the position until Daryl tugged at his arm.

"People are laughing at you," the boy whispered.

"Let them." The duke lifted his head and stared coldly around at the gawking, sniggering crowd. Eyes dropped; faces turned away. The duke returned his attention to a scarlet-faced Leslie.

"Blushing suits you," he said. "I shall have to make sure you have plenty of opportunity. And in case you have not learned your lesson: Impudence toward your long-suffering Benefactor will invariably be punished in exactly that manner."

The threat held Leslie silent. Drogo watched her sharply for a moment, and then, grinning unforgivably, turned to discuss the balloon flight with the younger girls.

The duke deposited the Endales at their great-aunt's door after regaling them with cream pastries and orgeat. To Leslie's combined relief and disappointment, he refused to come in, merely warning Leslie that he would call for her the following day and escort her to the boutique of a suitable modiste. "For you will admit," he said smugly, "that my taste in bonnets and . . . other things is faultless."

If Leslie had had any intention of refusing, this reference to the unacknowledged gifts would have been enough to render her amenable. She tried to voice her belated thanks for the duke's kindness, but he waved her stammered words away with an autocratic gesture.

"Tell me all about it tomorrow." He grinned, and strode back to his carriage.

"Our Benefactor!" sighed Hilary.

"He is doing very well by us, Leslie," said Meredith.

"He kissed Leslie," announced Daryl, just at the moment Weems opened the door for them.

Altogether a frustrating day, Leslie decided grimly.

Chapter 20

Leslie prepared for the ordeal early the next day. She had donned, again, the outfit the duke had chosen for her, Cameron having reinforced her own belief that it was the only suitable costume she possessed. While she resented the necessity of admitting to her arrogant Benefactor that he knew more about alamodality than any member of *her* family, such was indeed the truth, and she must admit to it with as good a grace as possible.

While Leslie was taking a final, restorative peek into the large mirror Cameron had installed the previous day, the dresser was busy with the reticule the duke had given Leslie. A delicate scent wafted into the room. The girl turned to look.

Cameron was just returning the lace handkerchief to the reticule. She now advanced upon Leslie, handed over the little purse, and proceeded to place a drop of perfume upon Leslie's wrists and at the base of her throat. To the girl's surprise, she also put a tiny dab behind each of Leslie's ears.

"Why in just those particular places?" the girl asked with honest curiosity.

Cameron eyed her sternly, and then, perceiving that the question was sincere, answered, "These are the places where a lady may expect to receive a gentleman's particular . . . attentions."

Leslie blushed a deep rose-pink, and one small hand went automatically to cover the base of her throat.

Cameron's hard gaze softened further. "Do not let any gentleman presume upon your good nature, milady," she said stiffly. "You need only smile—and say no."

And again Cameron was surprised, this time by the delightful smile she received from her little charge. "You are a wise woman, Cameron," Leslie said. " 'Smile and say no'! A veritable amulet against wicked men!"

So it was with the feeling of being well armored against attack that Leslie accompanied the splendidly dressed Drogo in his closed carriage with the ducal crest upon the panel. She was chatting lightly, quite priding herself upon her sophisticated bearing, when the wily creature attacked from a quite unexpected quarter.

"I had better warn you, Leslie," he said, in a voice that reminded her of Daryl at his most brotherly, "that we may encounter hostility in the salons we shall be visiting today."

"H-hostility?" quavered Leslie, the woman-of-the-world pose completely forgotten. "You are taking me where they will not wish to serve me?"

"Oh, no, child! *Eugenie*, and later, *Panache*, are two salons whose resources are only surpassed by the charm of their proprietors. No, child, the hostility of which I speak is to be expected from certain clients of theirs, elegant ladies of the ton, who, being a little older than yourself—" and he flashed her a knowing, boyish grin "—may resent your youthful charm and freshness."

Leslie was no fool. Immediately mistrustful of the boyish charm her difficult sponsor was piling on so thickly, she frowned a little as she tried to discover his motive in this about-face from arrogance to brotherly concern.

"Why should they resent me?" she said sharply. "We both know I am the veriest country bumpkin, a green girl without finish, whose only suitable garments were purchased by you."

"But perhaps *they* will not know that," suggested Drogo, now wearing his wide, white grin. "Or if they do, they may be envious of your . . . good fortune."

Leslie caught her breath. *Devil!* "You are saying they may be jealous of me because I am being sponsored by London's most famous rake?" she asked sweetly. "Surely they will be able to perceive that the Duke of Kenelm is far too—*old*—for me?"

The wolfish grin softened into a reluctant smile. "Little brat," said Drogo, in a more comfortable tone than he had yet used to address her. "I see you have much to learn."

In spite of which rather ominous pronouncement, he beguiled the rest of the drive with witty *on dits* and scandalous comments upon many of the gentlemen-on-the-strut they passed. When finally the carriage drew up before a neat yet unobtrusive little shop on Bond Street, Leslie could hardly wait to enter and behold the riches it no doubt contained. Nor was she disappointed. Madame Eugenie herself came out to serve so well-known a customer as the Duke of Kenelm. He introduced the two women, said that Lady Leslie required something quietly elegant for her introduction to the ton, and added that of course he had recommended *Eugenie*.

Two blissful hours later, a dazed Leslie was seated again in the ducal coach, beside a quietly smiling Drogo. She heaved a sigh of enormous content.

"If I live to be one hundred, I will never be able to thank you enough for today," breathed the girl, turning to her Benefactor with a glowing face.

Drogo was silent for an instant, his tawny-gold eyes a dark amber as they searched the ingenuous countenance raised to his. "But if I am too old for you now"—he quoted her earlier remark with a slightly twisted smile—"what will I be in a hundred years?"

"Oh, you knew I was just funning, paying you back for the way you were teasing me about your many conquests," Leslie chuckled.

"Oh, is that what I was doing?" asked Drogo.

"You know you were," laughed the girl. "You are forever teasing me! I must be an easy mark, being such a gape-seed! But Cameron is teaching me to recognize a dangerous male when I meet one, and you do not at all qualify!'' Had Leslie not been exhausted, and slightly intoxicated by the lovely garments they had chosen, she might have been more wary of her companion's touchy masculine pride.

"So that is what your formidable dresser is doing," mused the duke softly. "Can you tell me what she has taught you so far?"

Again the girl missed the warning signs. "Oh, yes!" she chuckled. "You put perfume on certain parts of your anatomy, and then you smile and say no—" She stopped abruptly, aware of the change in Drogo's expression.

Staring down at her now were the bright golden eyes of a hunting animal, fierce and beautiful and intent. A velvet growl sounded in her startled ears as two hard arms closed around her body.

"Shall I try to discover the parts of your anatomy you have perfumed to entice me?" murmured Drogo. "Here, perhaps? And here?" he said as he set his warm, hard lips against the sides of her throat. "And here?" He bent his shining golden head against her breast, smoothly pressing aside the neat folds of the redingote.

Leslie, who had gasped and closed her eyes at the first assault, now opened them widely at this invasion. As her whole body stiffened, Drogo lifted his head and stared down into her face arrogantly.

What he saw there gave him pause.

For perhaps the first time in his life, he looked into eyes that were completely open, welcoming, loving. Wide and innocent eyes that seemed to be adoring him even while he ravished her. Drogo felt a trembling begin deep inside his body. Almost with relief he lifted his head, put the girl back on her own side of the carriage, and said crisply, "I hope that will teach you not to tease your male companions. *Perfume on your anatomy*, indeed! Practice circumspection, ma'am, or you will find yourself in uncomfortable straits!"

"But Cameron told me to say no," murmured Leslie, greatly daring.

Drogo glared at her. "I saw very little evidence of reluctance in your behavior," he snapped. "And I did not hear the word *no*. On the contrary—!"

"I shall try to be more circumspect," whispered Leslie meekly. But her heart was singing.

The duke did not return to Cavendish Square for several days. The correct gifts arrived: a rare old book for Lady Bella, which sent her into raptures; a box full of pink roses for Leslie, through which she searched in vain for a message or even a card. For the children there were delightful toys and a huge box of sweets.

Everyone except Leslie was loud in the praise of their charming friend and Benefactor. Lady Bella disclosed that he had gotten invitations for herself and Leslie for the Grand Ball being given the following week by Lady Pentacle, whose enormous wealth was only rivaled by her husband's ancient name. Leslie felt a frightening chill of premonition.

"I must not go!" she whispered.

In the face of this social triumph, Lady Bella had no patience with missish vaporings. "Of course you will go," she said crisply. "And so shall I. Lord Pentacle owns the finest library in London—possibly in all of England. Do you think I will miss a chance to see it? Why should you not wish to go? You will be beautifully dressed, and you will meet presentable young men."

"I am afraid," breathed the girl.

Her great-aunt turned on her with annoyance. "If you fear to make a bumble-broth of the dancing, I can assure you that *Maître* Henri tells me you have learned your steps very prettily. You really do not need to talk much, since most young men would rather hear their own ramblings than the wittiest discussion of anything important. And as for your appearance—" she lifted her brows"—Cameron will do us both proud."

Leslie remained silent, not able to explain to her elated relative that the very thought of being under the critical gaze of the ton was terrifying to her. No doubt there would be a dozen of the duke's old flirts there, who would take pleasure in cutting down the green girl with whom Drogo Trevelyan had been saddled.

Above all—and least to be admitted—was the fear that gauche Leslie would betray her lack of town bronze before the critical eyes of Drogo's intimates, and make *him* a laughingstock.

The news that came two days before the Grand Ball did a little to reassure her.

Lady Bella came into the drawing room, where Leslie and Meredith were listening to Hilary perform on the pianoforte, which she did rather well, if very sentimentally. The elderly peeress interrupted the concert ruthlessly.

"Leslie! What joyous news! Apollo has cast his cloak about us! He intends to pick us up in his chariot and whisk us through the Heavens!"

Stunned, the Endales stared at their great-aunt. After a moment of waiting for them to express their pleasure, Lady Bella frowned at them. "I would have thought that you, Leslie, at least, would have been pleased to hear that Kenelm is going to escort us to the Pentacles' ball!"

Light dawned. Lady Bella had not favored them with too many classical references, and when she did, she recited them as part of an educational process. It was clear to Leslie now that her redoubtable relative had been nurturing a few fears of her own about their appearance at the Grand Ball. She would naturally feel much more confident on the arm of the most notable bachelor in London. The news gave Leslie a feeling of security, also. She began to smile.

"Apollo, is it? I had thought you considered the duke more in the light of a Don Juan. Or a Casanova?"

Lady Bella sniffed, but her real relief at the duke's offer was apparent.

So it was a relaxed and happy pair of ladies who came down to wait for their escort in the drawing room on the night of the Pentacles' Grand Ball. Lady Bella, flourishing under Cameron's eagle eye and superb skills, had never appeared to better advantage. Her dowager's turban was of soft mauve silk, exactly matching the flattering Empire-style gown Cameron had helped her choose. There was even a subtle shading of maquillage to brighten her old cheeks.

Leslie had stood entranced before the big mirror in her room for quite five minutes after Cameron had finished with her. Her white silk dress was one Drogo had chosen, of course, but it seemed to have acquired an added luster after the dresser had brushed the girl's hair into a softly feminine style and crowned the neat waves with a wreath of white roses.

Cameron refused to let Leslie wear any of the ornate jewelry Lady Bella offered, saying that the single white rose at her corsage was ornament enough for a debutante. The flower drew attention to the girl's gently rounded breasts. The soft silk lovingly followed the line of the slender figure to the small waist, and then rustled out into a gentle fullness to the floor. Leslie could not decide if she was pleased by the radiant simplicity of her costume, or if she was fearful that it would appear childish amid tonight's sophisticated company.

The duke, announced by Weems, entered the drawing room and paused for a moment just within the door to stare hard at the two ladies who awaited him. Leslie watched his expression, hoping to read in it some satisfaction at her appearance. Drogo advanced and bent over Lady Bella's extended hand.

"Superb, Lady Beautiful," he said, translating her name. " 'Ripeness is all.' "

Lady Bella, bridling with pleasure, turned to indicate her great-niece proudly.

The duke walked over to bow to Leslie, his eyes anywhere but on her glowing, expectant face. The girl thought she read something hard and remote in his manner, and her heart misgave her. What had she done to bring this *distance* between them? she thought anxiously, looking down at the tawny-gold head bowed before her. And then the duke straightened, and stared at her with eyes of amber-gold. Leslie caught her breath. No human should be so . . . so *beautiful*, she decided with despair.

Since the duke said nothing, merely held her hand and stared into her face, Leslie finally said, "Do I disappoint you, Your Grace?"

Slowly Drogo shook his head, his eyes fixed on her delicate sweetness. "No, fledgling, you don't disappoint me. Other things, yes. But not disappointment." He seemed to recollect himself, and continued with his usual mocking smile, "My quotation which I rehearsed for *you*, child—knowing that I was entering the Halls of Athene!" with a teasing grin at Lady Bella, "—*'She doth teach the torches to burn bright!'* "

The old bluestocking nodded benignly. "Appropriate, and flattering, Kenelm! *Romeo and Juliet*," she added kindly, for Leslie's benefit.

The girl was too busy wondering if he really meant it, or if that was the way all beaux addressed the ladies, to notice the very intent gaze Drogo was focusing upon her small, blushing countenance.

After such an exciting beginning, the rest of the evening could have been a disaster without Leslie noticing the fact. It was, however, a veritable triumph for the ladies under the escort of the Duke of Kenelm. Lady Bella was aware that she had never been so courted by the ton, and determined to explain to green Leslie exactly how fortunate she was in arriving under the shield of the golden duke. Leaders of the beau monde, who would have ignored a country nobody, were all gracious smiles to the duke's young guest. Young bloods cast a searching eye over the girl who had appeared from nowhere on the arm of Drogo Trevelyan, while impecunious younger sons hovered hopefully, muttering questions about her background to one another.

Lady Bella, hot after a sight of the precious holding, pestered her host into showing her his magnificent library. His wife had to send their butler after the two bibliophiles when they had been gone for a full hour.

"With anyone but Lady Endale I might have worried," she confided to her bosom bow, Countess de Lieven. "But Bella's sole interest is in Pen's books!"

"The niece is rather an ingenuous little bud," mused the countess. "Shall I send her a voucher for Almack's?"

Lady Pentacle pursed her lips. "She seems harmless, and the family is an old one. A great deal of money, I believe, but it all goes to the earl—a boy of nine. I wonder why Drogo is playing the cavalier?"

The ladies exchanged glances. It did not occur to either of them that the Duke of Kenelm might have serious intentions.

One rather nasty little incident occurred toward the end of the evening. Leslie was seated in a pretty bower of plants and shrubs, a charming place from which to observe the gowns of the dancers. She had been firmly placed there by Drogo, and told to sit quietly while he fetched her a glass of champagne.

"If you are asked to dance—" his baleful glance slid over a few hovering young males "—you will say that you are waiting for me. Am I clear, child?"

Leslie experienced a pang of annoyance. Why did he continue to call her *child*? Surely she was holding her own among the debutantes, even if she was far from the glamour of the real diamonds? Still, she reminded herself, this exciting evening was a gift from the duke. She agreed with Lady Bella that, without his sponsorship, the night would have been very different. So she smiled up at him with her sweetest smile.

"Yes, Drogo."

"Brat," said the duke, and went off to the buffet.

The two fashionably dressed females who had been lingering on the far side of the greenery now moved a little closer and began to speak in voices that carried very clearly, as they were well aware.

"Who *is* that odd little creature Drogo is saddled with?" asked Lady Sybil Cawden.

Her friend and fellow conspirator, Miss Tottie Deene, gave an artificially melodious laugh. "Oh, she is some country ninnyhammer whose estate borders on his. I imagine the poor man was fairly dragooned into squiring her tonight!"

"He seems to be getting away from her as often as he is able," vouchsafed Sybil. "Poor Drogo! The silly little gawk is clinging to him as though she thought he was serious!"

A duet of laughter chimed at the absurdity of this idea.

At first, Leslie had felt all the chagrin and despair her tormentors had hoped for. Her face became pale, her eyes darkened with humiliation. And then, glancing sideways through the shrouding greenery, she caught a curiously smug exchange of smiles between the two young women. At once her shoulders squared and her small jaw set itself firmly.

A few minutes later, Drogo came toward her through the crowd, his golden head shining under the lights of the chandeliers. He was carrying a glass of champagne in each hand, searching for Leslie. His expression revealed nothing, but the closed look softened into a smile as he sighted the girl. He handed her one of the glasses.

"To our great adventure, Leslie! Success and happiness."

Leslie's charming gurgle of laughter surprised him. For one thing, it was louder than he would have expected. Had someone else given the little filly champagne already?

And then Leslie, carefully not looking in the direction of the two gossips, said clearly, "Oh, darling Drogo! You are a naughty creature! You are so persistent! I have already told you I was going to say no to all your proposals, however charmingly you keep presenting them to me."

She hoped the two conspirators could not see Drogo's face, for the expression of shock and alarm that had crossed it as he heard her coy speech was a dead giveaway. But almost before she had caught the expression, it was gone, and a devilish grin warned her there would be a reckoning very soon. To make sure he didn't challenge her on the spot, and thus ruin her ploy, Leslie tossed off the champagne in two gulps, rose, and . . . fell into Drogo's hastily opened arms.

"It must be the champagne," she murmured against his pristine shirt. "I have never had it before."

Drogo continued to hold her firmly against his chest, in an embrace that began to draw curious, and some frankly disapproving, glances. She was glad she could not observe, from her present position, whatever expression now blazed in his tawny eyes, for his voice was the harsh purr of a tiger against her ear.

"You had better have a very good explanation for this imbroglio, Leslie!" he warned. "Now, *follow my lead!*" He held her gently away from him as he explained to the avid group clustering around them, "Lady Leslie has become faint! The heat has overcome her! I must take her out of the ballroom. Will someone please send a footman for Lady Bella Endale? I am sure she can be found in the *library!*"

This last was said with such an arch smile that even the guests who did not know the old bluestocking found themselves laughing. Drogo recalled Leslie to her duty with a shrewd pinch, and she obligingly collapsed against his big frame and permitted herself to droop against his shoulder.

A few moments later he had her in the spacious entry hall, which was indeed much cooler than the ballroom with its dozen blazing chandeliers. He set her down hard on a wooden bench, disregarding her muffled protest.

"Better keep silent," he warned her, sotto voce. "We are not out of the woods yet!"

Indeed, at that moment, summoned by an alert staff, Lady Pentacle bore down upon them like a ship under full sail. Lady Bella followed close behind her, her old face anxious. Drogo was quick to reassure them both.

"Our little girl was overcome by the heat," he said softly, one minatory hand tightly grasping Leslie's shoulder. He treated his concerned hostess to a seductive smile. "Or perhaps she was too greatly impressed by the elegance of your delightful party, ma'am," he told his gratified hostess. "Lady Leslie is a dear child, but, between us, Lady Pentacle, she's never seen anything in the country to equal tonight's squeeze! A resounding success!"

He had gestured to the butler as he bore Leslie into the hallway. The man had not failed him. He came forward to announce that His Grace's carriage was at the door, and to present His Grace's hat and the ladies' cloaks. Within a remarkably short time the three were seated within the carriage, being jolted along the cobblestones toward Cavendish Square.

"What was that all about?" demanded Lady Bella suspiciously.

Leslie smothered a grin, and waited for Drogo's reply.

The duke surprised them both. His voice was as smooth and hard and cold as marble as he said, "It is better that you do not know, Lady Bella, until I have cleared the matter with your great-niece."

The old woman peered through the gloom at Leslie, and then at the big man who sat facing them. Whatever she saw in their faces, she was wise enough not to press the matter further. If Leslie had gotten herself into a brangle, then how fortunate for them all that Kenelm had been present and willing to carry the incident off so successfully!

Under her modish cloak, Leslie shivered a little at the thought of the coming reckoning.

Chapter 21

When Weems ushered the little party into the well-lighted hallway, Lady Bella cast a quick, assessing glance at her two companions.

"I suppose I must let you settle whatever is at issue between you," she said grudgingly. "However, I advise you to be sensible and quick. As Macbeth said, 'If it were done when 'tis done, then 'twere well It were done quickly.' " Observing their puzzled frowns, she admitted, "Oh, well, I never did feel really comfortable with that remark myself. I thought it apropos because Macbeth was planning to murder his king, and Kenelm is acting as though he wanted to murder you, Leslie. Think twice, Kenelm! Whatever she did at the ball, however annoying she is, she has a certain *quality*."

The old bluestocking gave Leslie a warm smile, and then went on up the stairway, formally preceded by one of her footmen bearing a candelabrum. Drogo bowed silently, his expression unreadable.

Leslie hurried ahead of him into the drawing room. When his voice sounded harshly at her very shoulder, she jumped with alarm. Drogo's hand came down heavily on her arm.

"You will now explain that provocative little scene at the ball."

There was so much tightly harnessed anger in his voice that Leslie knew only complete honesty would serve.

"There were these two women," she began, and had to

clear her throat. She could not force herself to raise her eyes to meet his.

"Yes?" The syllable was uncompromising.

"They were saying cruel things about me, and at first I was . . . shocked and hurt." The girl paused, but no sound came from the big man looming so threateningly beside her. She went on, "Then I noticed that they were speaking very distinctly, as though they . . . wished me to hear them."

Drogo said sharply, "Two women? What did they look like?"

"I really didn't notice," began Leslie crossly.

"Well?" Drogo's impatient question quickly unloosened her tongue.

"One was short and rather plump," she said hastily. "She had on a red dress which was too tight for her. The other was very beautiful, and was wearing a gold dress which exactly matched her hair."

"For someone who *really didn't notice*," Drogo said mockingly, "you describe Sybil and Tottie very well! Tottie Deene is the plump redhead, and the gorgeous blond female is Lady Sybil Cawden. Both of them have been casting out lures to me all Season, but I am too wily a bird to be caught in such dull little traps!"

"The beauty has a very harsh voice," announced Leslie.

"So it was to get revenge on a pair of vicious little cats that you intimated to all the ton that I had been paying you my addresses?" demanded the duke.

At last Leslie's gaze came up to meet his piercing stare. A bright blush of color flowed into her cheeks, but her eyes held his steadily. She even essayed a smile. "But you are too wily a bird to be caught in that dull little trap, are you not?" She quoted his own words back to him as bravely as she could.

"You will stop playing childish games and tell me exactly what was said," her tormentor instructed her.

"The beauty asked her friend for the name of the odd little creature you were saddled with. The fat one laughed and said I was an unknown—a country ninnyhammer I believe was her charming phrase—whom you had been forced to bring with you tonight.''

''Knowing full well that I am *never* forced to do anything I do not wish to do,'' said Drogo silkily.

''Are you not?'' Leslie showed her surprise. ''Never? How *freeing* for you! Most people do a great many things they would rather not!''

''Was that all that was said?'' Drogo returned her sternly to the subject at hand.

''Oh, no!'' Leslie was surprised to discover that the pain and humiliation she had felt were somehow dissolving under the big man's determined inquisition. ''The beauty expressed her sorrow that you had had me foisted upon you: 'Poor Drogo,' I believe she called you. And added that I would spoil your evening, acting as though you were serious about me, silly gawk that I was, and shame you by clinging to you as though you were my whole dependence and delight!''

Her active imagination had carried her on this verbal flight, one worthy of Hilary at her most dramatic, Leslie realized with a smothered grin. She glanced up to share the joke with the duke, and found the golden eyes blazing down at her in a positive fury.

''How *dared* she!'' he gritted.

Leslie was startled out of her good humor. ''But you have said, or at least implied, the same or worse!'' she protested.

''That was my duty as your mentor,'' Drogo said stiffly. ''I am obliged to warn and . . . uh . . . instruct you. You are such a green girl, and the ton is so cruelly unforgiving!''

Leslie was unwilling to allow the duke this easy excuse for his mocking behavior. ''You have even suggested that I might pay you back for your help to Daryl by becoming your mistress! Meredith explained it to me,'' she added, catching his shocked expression. ''The 'cozy little establishment,' '' She reminded him of his offer.

The duke's face was dark with angry confusion. ''I was only teasing you,'' he explained untruthfully. ''You knew that!'' Assessing her piquant countenance fiercely, he caught the sparkle of laughter in the big blue eyes, and his expression hardened and became wary. "You learn town ways very easily, I begin to perceive," he said stiffly. "Present my compliments to Lady Bella. I shall remove my . . . ah . . . dissolute person before I contaminate your maidenly vicinity," he said too formally. "You and the boy are safe now. It is unlikely we shall have to meet again.''

Their next meeting was two days later.

A flustered little maidservant came into the bedroom where Cameron was preparing her charge for the day, and recited rapidly, "The Duke of Kenelm requests the pleasure of a conference with Lady Leslie immediately! And he sounds *awful mad*!'' she ended in a frightened gulp.

Cameron stilled the convulsive movement of her charge.

"You may take a message back to His Grace," she said calmly. "Tell him that Lady Leslie will see him in the drawing room in fifteen minutes. That is all," she told the staring maid. As the latter whisked out the door, Cameron resumed the careful brush-stroking of her mistress's hair. She addressed Leslie quietly.

."Whatever he wants, it can't be pleasant, or he wouldn't have terrified the maid. Therefore, you must be prepared for the encounter. Your best morning dress, I think. And this new hairstyle." She began to twist the lustrous strands into a simple yet striking design.

"I had a dream last night," Cameron said. "In it, I saw you walking down a dark stairway with danger at your heels. You were wearing a silk dress exactly the color of your eyes; little blue slippers moved in and out under the hem of your gown. And at the bottom of the stairs . . . true love was waiting!''

Hypnotized by the deep, bardic tones and the soothing brush strokes, Leslie watched her image in the mirror wonderingly.

I am . . . pretty! she thought. And then: *true love!*

"And then what?" she whispered.

121

"That was it," said Cameron shortly. "I shall create the coiffure. You must do the rest."

However, a few minutes later, Cameron opened the small box she had left on the dressing table. She removed a brush and a small pot, and began industriously to work on Leslie's face.

Maquillage! thought Leslie with guilty delight. The paint that had made Lady Bella appear so much younger and brighter, and that had given Leslie herself a becoming flush to conceal pallid cheeks. Was that what Cameron had meant by "preparing for the encounter"? Of course it was! Armor against all comers!

"I shall wear this coiffure as though it were a helmet," she promised.

Cameron, looking a little confused, got on with applying the maquillage. When all was to her liking, she helped Leslie into a charming morning dress and pushed her firmly toward the door.

And thus it was that Lady Leslie, looking remarkably self-possessed and prettier than the duke remembered, came quietly into the drawing room exactly fifteen minutes after her message.

The duke was striding up and down in a manner that made the spacious room appear too small. He was in a fine temper, and lost no time venting it upon the wide-eyed girl.

"The half was not told me," he began the attack. "When you were relating the details of the encounter at the ball to me in this very room that night, you neglected to supply me with several rather important facts. Slipped your mind, no doubt!"

Leslie stared. What was troubling the arrogant male now? She had told him everything, even built it up a little as Hilary so often did.

And then it struck her that she was getting rather tired of the man's constant criticism and misdirected anger. Who did he think he was, to rant at her in this manner whenever it pleased him?

"If you have something to say—some crime to charge me with—I suggest you do so and then leave this house!"

Leslie snapped, with a fury that met and challenged his own.

The girl's defiance seemed to give the duke momentary pause, but almost at once he was bearing down upon her with all the force of his masculine rage.

"I suppose I have you to thank for the rumors that are circulating throughout the ton? The clubs were abuzz with them yesterday. I entered White's to be greeted by a sudden silence and then an artificial prattle of nonsense, which failed to mask the avid curiosity of every man in the room. I, Kenelm, was an *on dit*!"

Meeting his accusing glare with one of her own, Leslie cried out, "Do you seek to blame me for the bad manners of your wretched companions? I warrant you those men have talked about you before, and will again! I am not unaware of your reputation as a . . . a . . ." Facing those blazing golden eyes, the girl paused.

Drogo's face was now white with fury. "As a *what*, Madame Holier-than-Thou? Lady Prim and Proper! Fine words from a female who has just titillated London with the announcement of our approaching nuptials!"

"You are insane!" breathed Leslie. "Or else your sense of your own consequence is so overweening that you see interest where none is present, and cannot imagine any woman able to resist your . . . your *nonexistent charms*!" she finished most unfairly.

Unwisely, too, as became frighteningly clear.

The Duke of Kenelm, who had never voluntarily touched another human being except in the gymnasium or in amorous dalliance, now stepped forward and jerked the maddening little creature hard against his chest. The action knocked the breath from her slender body momentarily, and shocked her so that she stared, speechless, up into his molten eyes. She was so small against his massive frame, and so obviously enraged by his behavior, that an involuntary grin twitched at the duke's lips. Fully aware that it would enrage her further, he said in tones of honeyed disdain, "What was it that Sybil named you the other night?

'A paltry little thing? Oh, no. It was 'a country ninnyhammer'.''

"That was Tottie," corrected the girl, trying for justice even in her anger. "Your dear friend Sybil said I was a *silly little gawk*. Not an elegant phrase for one who pretends to good *ton*."

The truth was that Leslie was experiencing emotions and physical responses she had never known before. Her whole body was being filled with a strange, exciting warmth, which was radiating, she decided, from those portions of her anatomy that were directly in contact with the duke's massive form. Strange. And interesting, she had to acknowledge. She made a slight wriggling movement with her body, merely to test the properties of the unusual phenomenon, of course.

A warning masculine growl from Drogo's chest vibrated against Leslie's ear. "What do you think you are doing, wench?" muttered the beleaguered nobleman. His own anger, in the last few moments reduced to an unfamiliar mixture of indulgence and annoyance, was suddenly swept away completely in a blaze of sexual awareness. What was the little vixen up to, wiggling so seductively in his arms? *Was* she trying to seduce him? Promising himself that he would have a serious discussion with the little wretch very shortly, the duke clutched the slender body closer in his arms and bent his tawny head to kiss those soft pink lips.

Leslie, who had by now forgotten the question, the answer, and even her own name, accepted and returned the kiss with fevered delight. It was *so long* since she had felt the comforting security of a pair of heavy masculine arms, the lulling warmth of a hard masculine chest! Papa had been an affectionate man, and there had been no dearth of hugs and kisses in the family. Papa . . .

But this was *not* Papa! This man whose very scent was subtly exciting, a combination of spices and clean linen, whose hard arms and warm body were definitely not paternal! The girl drew in a sustaining breath of the exciting aroma and then leaned back against the firm grip that was binding her.

The move had an interesting result. Hard lips came down again against her own, crushing, demanding. When they finally released her mouth, Leslie was almost without thought. Dimly she heard her own voice asking, "What is that scent you are using, Drogo? It is . . . quite intoxicating."

There was a moment of stunned silence, and then the low growl of male laughter rumbled against her body. "Are you saying I make you drunk?"

"I am saying," stammered the bewildered girl, "that you had better release me before I do something . . . silly."

"Like what?" demanded her captor, highly interested.

Like falling deeper into love with you than I am now, thought the girl. *Like throwing my arms around you and kissing you until* you *feel this intoxicating magic!* Then the pain of realizing her own folly brought self-disgust. "Like making a complete fool of myself," she told him, "and proving to your sophisticated friends that I am in truth the stupid country bumpkin they named me."

The girl's eyes still met his, but her expression was cold and closed. Drogo realized that he had lost the moment that had so strongly stirred him. As a result, he became angry again—at the girl, at whatever had frozen her youthful warmth, at himself. He stared into her face, his anger reviving.

"We have not yet established your part in this latest imbroglio," he said cruelly. "Was it indeed you who set the rumors to flying? That the impregnable fortress of Kenelm had surrendered at last to a green girl—"

Leslie had taken all she intended to from the arrogant duke.

"Use the wits you were born with, Kenelm," she said abruptly. "Whom do I know in the beau monde? What opportunity have I had to tattle about my conquests? What conquests?" She drew a steadying breath, glaring at her hateful tormentor. "Look among your charming friends to find the source of the rumors which so distress you. I give you my word I have not even talked to anyone who might have spread so absurd a tale!"

She turned away abruptly, her shoulders stiff with wounded pride and something else that she was reluctant to identify. She had nearly reached the door when it was flying open to admit a very worried Lady Bella.

"Where is the earl?" she demanded. "His tutor says he has missed his lessons this morning."

"Surely that is not an unusual occurrence with a small boy?" asked Drogo, coming forward to bow over the old lady's hand. "Dear Lady Bella, how attractive you look in that pink bergère! Now you must not worry over Daryl, ma'am. Boys of his age are forever running off to see the world. He'll be back as soon as he gets hungry, I promise."

His voice was reassuring, so kind and rallying, in fact, that Leslie stared openly, surprised that such compassion could issue from that cynical mouth.

Lady Bella smiled, but her eyes still mirrored her alarm. "The threats against Daryl's life . . . ?" she offered tentatively.

"I shall of course remain here until he returns," said Drogo calmly. "Perhaps it is time we thought of sending him to a good preparatory school, ma'am. I am sure his papa would have his name down somewhere."

"Eton," said Leslie shortly. "But he is too young yet."

Both her great-aunt and Drogo looked at her with surprise. Leslie made no effort to explain further. Instead she told them, "I think I should go out to look for Daryl in the park." The square was centered by a small, enclosed garden with many tall trees. "Daryl loves to climb," she explained stiffly.

"Then we shall send out two footmen to scour the bushes," suggested Drogo in a tone Leslie felt was too casually unconcerned. She was preparing to deliver a lecture on the gravity of the situation when the boy himself appeared in the doorway.

He was dusty, disheveled, and grinning broadly. "Oh, Leslie, you will never believe the adventure I have had! He was going to give me a puppet if I went with him to his home, and then the young man almost ran us down in the *most famous* contraption, and he gave me a ride on it and brought me back home.'' The boy sighed his satisfaction. "But I wish I had gotten the puppet as well,'' he concluded regretfully.

Lady Bella rolled her eyes to heaven and walked toward the bellpull to summon a footman. Leslie, hugging the unrepentant Daryl rather fiercely to her bosom, met the enigmatic gaze of the duke with a small frisson of alarm. She must get to the bottom of Daryl's tangled tale as soon as possible, because it was plain that the boy had gone cheerfully off with not one, but two strangers, either of whom might have been agents of March Wardell. But something about Drogo Trevelyan's attitude bothered her. He had seemed so *sure* that nothing bad could have happened to the young earl! Was his lack of real concern just a part of a cold nature? Or did he have some sort of information?

The girl tried in vain to read the handsome, enigmatic countenance.

Chapter 22

The Duke of Kenelm took urbane leave of his hostess and his fellow peer, and departed. Without, Leslie thought resentfully, having the courage to stay and finish our argument, or the courtesy to ask my pardon for his wicked suspicions.

"And now, Daryl," she said in a no-nonsense voice, "I should like the full story of your adventure today."

The earl looked a trifle discomfited. "Hadn't I better wash up first?" he asked hopefully. "You have always instructed me to present myself tidily before guests."

Leslie smothered a grin. "This matter is of greater importance than a social nicety. And besides, I am merely your long-suffering sister, not your guest." She allowed her stern expression to soften. "You are not a dunce, Daryl! You cannot have forgotten that Wardell twice tried to . . . hurt you." Her voice broke a little on the euphemism.

Her brother stared at her soberly. "Kill me, you mean." He frowned. "Yes, I must admit I had forgotten that when I walked out this morning to see the sights. Oh, Leslie! Sometimes I wish so hard just to be free again, to run out into the meadows and climb trees and ride my horse across the fields—"

Leslie's conscience smote her. She *had* forgotten that the heir was a boy of nine, and would wish for—and *need*—all the childish games natural to that age. Cooped up in a musty old house in a quiet square in London, with no other children to play with, of course he would wish to get out and explore this new world! She caught him close in a brief hard hug.

"Drogo Trevelyan suggests you might want to go to a school with other boys of your age, share the games and—" with a smile to match his sudden hopeful grin "—begin a formal course of studies to prepare you for your duties to the family."

Even that rather daunting conclusion did not wipe out the sparkle of excitement and interest in Daryl's eyes.

"I think I should like that, Leslie. Would I fit in with the others?" he asked wistfully. "I have never really had any other boys to play with." He stared into her loving countenance. "Would I see you and Meredith and Hilary now and then?"

Leslie's heart swelled with love for the small, dusty, gallant figure. "Of course! Could you imagine us *staying away*? My only fear would be that you would come to dread the sight of such constant visitors as we shall be, and fear the teasing of your schoolmates over such devoted sisters!"

Daryl chuckled, and gave her a pert look. "They would more likely be begging to meet you all," he laughed. "I might do a profitable business bartering for introductions!"

"Daryl!" exclaimed his sister. Surely, at his age, the boy should not have so much worldly sophistication. It was indeed high time that she placed her precocious little brother under suitable male guidance! Which reminded her that today's dangerous adventure had still to be dealt with.

"Now you will tell me, if you please, exactly what happened today. For you must admit—" she softened the command with a smile "—your brief account left much to be desired."

Daryl's face creased into a wide grin. "It was beyond anything great! I had just gone out for a few moments' exercise before my session with old Molly—that is, *Mr.* Molliford," he amended hastily, catching Leslie's frown. "Well, he is stuffy and long-winded and—oh, well, I was trying to nip out and miss him," the boy confessed sheepishly. "He hardly knows whether I'm there or not, most days. Got his nose stuck in some book—'' Leslie's raised eyebrows brought him firmly back to the subject.

"I went into the park across the street, and the first thing I saw was this splendid Punch-and-Judy show. Leslie, I had never *seen* a Punch-and-Judy show before! The man was so *funny*, he made me laugh and laugh. He told me all about the puppets, and even let me hold them. And *then* he said he'd give me a set for my very own, if I would wish to come with him to his house and get them. . . .''

Noticing the look of shock on Leslie's face, Daryl paused. "I shouldn't have gone with him," he said heavily.

"Were there other children watching the show?" Leslie asked gently.

"No. But then there aren't any other children here in the square, are there? I haven't seen any."

Definitely the duke was right, thought Leslie sadly. It was time for Daryl to enter a world proper for his sex, age, and station in life. Giving silent thanks for his safe return, she said calmly, repeating one of his own favorite phrases, "And then what?"

Daryl's expression brightened. "The most famous thing! The puppet-man and I were walking along a rather crowded street when we heard a loud noise; in fact, it was a real commotion, like a fair on the village green. And who should come barreling down the road but a young man on a *machine* with wooden wheels! It made a fine racket, I can tell you!" Daryl nodded his satisfaction. "The fellow was grinning and shouting: 'Make way for the Dray-see-en!' or some such name. You would have thought it *prime*, just as I did! There were these two wooden wheels, you see, and a sort of saddle slung between them, and the fellow pushed himself along with his feet. It was *splendacious*!"

"So of course you asked the young man if you might try it?" said Leslie with sisterly resignation.

"No. He pulled up beside us and asked *me* if I wished a ride," was the surprising answer.

"Was he a friend of the puppet-man?"

Daryl shook his head. "I don't think so. The puppet-man caught at my shoulder and said I mustn't risk my neck on such a totty-headed contraption. And then the young man said *it was plain as the nose on the puppet-man's face*—and that was a good joke, because the man had an enormous snout, Leslie—*that he was an old spoilsport*. And before anyone could stop him," concluded the boy with relish, "the fellow had me up on the saddle before him and was wheeling down the street. And the first thing I knew, we were bouncing up in front of Aunt Bella's door." He sighed. "It was great fun, but I wish I had had a chance to collect the puppets! Leslie, do you think . . . ?"

"I shall see that you get some," promised the girl. A small price to pay for the boundless relief of having the earl back safe with his family. "You must understand, Daryl, that there are men—Wardell and others like him—who would be glad to have you in their home so they could make you do whatever they wished." It was an awkward business, trying to warn the boy without terrifying him. What a shame to seal off that lovely spontaneity under a hard shell of wary distrust! Leslie began to understand a little the rigid facade a man like the Duke of Kenelm must be obliged to present to the world.

The Duke! Leslie recalled his utter lack of anxiety when Daryl was reported missing. Could it be that the youth on the wheeled machine was an agent of his? Surely the encounter could not have been entirely fortuitous. To pick one small boy out of a streetful, to offer him a ride, in fact, to insist that he ride. Feeling confused, and yet a great deal more friendly toward her arrogant Benefactor, the girl resolved to confront him with the question when next they met.

At that very moment, Drogo Trevelyan was receiving a report from the young cousin of his closest acquaintance, Kevin O'Dare. Young Patrick was a cheerful, vigorous giant who was blessed with more bottom than brains. He boasted that he would accept—and indeed had accepted—any challenge or wager proposed to him. This amiable idiot had been recruited by the duke to ride a certain contraption lately brought over to England from France. It had two wooden wheels, ranged one behind the other, and joined by a saddlelike seat. The vehicle, the invention of Baron Karl de Drais de Sauerbrun, was known as a *draisine*, and was propelled by the rider pushing both feet on the ground, either at once or one after another. Kevin had imported one as a joke, and dared his young cousin to ride it through London. When Drogo had observed this occasion, he was struck by a thought.

If the green girl was correct, and her wicked cousin was truly plotting to eliminate the young earl, then perhaps a better watch than that provided by an elderly bluestocking and a country chit might be in order. So he commissioned Patrick, who had nothing better to do, and had quite fallen in love with the absurd vehicle, to lurk about in the tree-shaded park at Cavendish Square with it, and follow if any attempt was made to abduct the little earl.

Luckily, the attempt was made within two days of the watch being set up. Patrick's interest in both the vehicle and the young nobleman probably would not have survived a longer waiting period. As it was, he had fulfilled his duty nobly, and was now being feted with an excellent brandy by his employer.

"Next time, make it a girl," he suggested, raising his glass to his cousin and the duke. "For me to follow, I mean."

"I have not the least doubt you can find your own girls, you young Irish devil," said Drogo. "Was there anything particularly noticeable about the kidnapper?"

Patrick guffawed. "He'd a nose as big as—a *cannon*, but that didn't make a holy man out of him," joked the young Irishman.

Both other men raised patient eyebrows at this display of childish punning.

"Not a gentleman, you would say?" pressed Drogo.

"A regular cutpurse, I would hazard. A very queer customer," agreed Patrick, savoring the brandy.

Drogo nodded decisively. "I think I had better have a little talk with someone in authority at Bow Street," he said softly.

Both of the other men gave him instant attention. Then Kevin asked, "You think it a serious threat?"

Drogo nodded.

"Then I shall come with you," decided Kevin. "Otherwise you are likely to wind up in the cells yourself. Your terrible reputation, you know!"

Chapter 23

The following morning Leslie rose early, supervised the breakfast of her siblings, and saw poor Daryl firmly into the library to his tutor. With a whispered promise to rescue him for a run through the park later, she closed the door upon his exasperated little face.

She was just crossing the hall to plan the day with her sisters when the knocker resounded. Weems, smiling benevolently in her direction, went to open the front door. Drogo Trevelyan, looking very much the man-about-town, stood upon the threshold holding a dainty bouquet of daisies.

With pleased delight and resentment battling for control, Leslie moved slowly toward the guest.

"Come in, Your Grace." She managed a formal little curtsy. "Have you had breakfast yet? May we offer you a cup of tea or coffee?"

Drogo's grin showed the girl that he was well aware of her waspish intention to suggest that his visit was unfashionably early.

"Thank you, Lady Leslie, I have already broken my fast," he said condescendingly. "I have been busy about your brother's affairs this morning."

Stricken with guilt—as the rogue meant her to be—Leslie silently led the way into the drawing room. There Drogo handed her the small posy with a grin.

"I thought the . . . ah . . . marguerites suitable," he began, mockingly.

"Because I am a green country girl?" demanded Leslie. Then she recollected the announced purpose of his visit, and controlled her temper. "Have you something to tell me about Daryl?" she asked, quietly.

Drogo seated himself on a comfortable sofa and indicated the space beside him. Leslie's brows moved upward; surely he was not proposing to indulge in a little dalliance so early in the morning.

Drogo read her expression easily. He chuckled. "No, my dear child, I have neither the intention nor the desire to explore your charms today. Perhaps on another, less formal occasion. . . ?" The fellow gave her his most devilish grin.

Leslie understood that he was just playing with her, *teasing. If only he really meant it!* the girl thought, and was immediately angry at herself. "What did you wish to tell us?" she asked as calmly as possible.

"I have alerted the officials at Bow Street as to the threats against the earl's life," he began quietly, all trace of laughter gone. "They inform me that I shall need—or they will—rather more concrete evidence. They have agreed to detail three of their men on eight-hour duty around the clock, to keep surveillance on this house from the park. And I," he added casually, "shall be persuading Weems to let me send one of my own grooms to the mews to keep watch from the stables. Rather sensible coverage, I think." His tone invited her agreement.

Leslie was almost overcome with gratitude. The duke was indeed behaving as their Benefactor, as Hilary had so emotionally named him. What other mere acquaintance would have gone to such lengths to protect a boy who was, after all, little more than a neighbor to him? She tried to express her gratitude, but the duke was suddenly remote and formal, and brushed aside her thanks with a courtly gesture.

"And now if I may pay my respects to Lady Bella?"

It was Leslie's turn to grin naughtily. "Would you like Weems to escort you up to her bedchamber?" she asked pertly. "Oh, here he is!" she said as the butler entered

135

followed by a footman bearing a tray. "Weems, His Grace wishes to—"

"Present his compliments to Lady Bella, and request an audience at her convenience later today," finished Drogo smoothly, but his glance at the smiling girl promised stern reprisals in the future.

Nodding gravely, Weems watched as the footman placed the tray upon a small table near Leslie. Then the two servants left the room.

"You are now supposed to ask for my preferences, pour me a restorative cup, and offer the—" Drogo scanned the plate of tiny pastries with a shudder "—ugh! Lady Bella must have a French chef in her kitchen!"

Leslie nodded, still smiling. "Roland. The children adore him—or his sweets."

Shuddering, Drogo accepted a cup of fragrant coffee and sipped warily. His shoulders relaxed. "Excellent," he judged, and drank the contents, holding out the empty cup with a challenging smile.

Leslie refilled it. Then she took a deep breath. "Your Grace—Drogo," she amended, catching his sudden frown, "we must talk! There is so much—"

The door of the drawing room opened to reveal a worried-looking Weems.

"Mr. March Wardell," he intoned. "And Mr. Charles Ruby."

March Wardell strode confidently into the room, followed by a sharp-faced man in neat black with an archaic-looking white stock. The heir ignored Drogo's presence entirely, fastening his expressionless small dark eyes threateningly on the girl's white face.

"You have led me a pretty chase, running off with the earl in this reprehensible fashion," he began, without giving the girl an opportunity to say anything. "Have you no knowledge of the risks you took, stealing away that child so thoughtlessly? You could have gotten him killed! Well, I am his legal guardian, and I have come, with Lawyer Ruby, to take the child back to his own home and proper guardian."

"Mr. Wardell, I presume?" asked the duke coolly.

Wardell swung his heavy torso around to discover the source of the interruption. He did not seem too impressed by the elegantly dressed fellow who had thrust himself into what obviously must be a private discussion.

"We'll excuse you, sir, whoever you are," he said unpleasantly. "This happens to be family business, and I'm pressed for time." His glance went back to dwell on Leslie's pale countenance.

"I," said Drogo in a voice of icy steel, "am Daryl's neighbor, and his father's friend. I am Kenelm."

The lawyer was regarding the duke with wary alarm. March Wardell had no such qualms. His hostility became a sneer. "Kenelm? You're the dissolute son of that crazy old psalm-singer, are you? Daryl has made an offer for your tumbledown mansion. See Ruby here about it, but do it later. We are busy now." He presented his shoulder to the duke, returning to the attack on the girl.

Lawyer Ruby, who knew a little more about Drogo Trevelyan than his client appeared to, was agape with shock at Wardell's faux pas.

Reprisal came swiftly. "I believe I must resent your manner, sir," Drogo said coldly. "Also your person. Both are offensive to any man of breeding." He advanced upon the startled heir, lifted one strong white hand, and struck Wardell hard on the cheek. "If you will name your seconds? Mr. Kevin O'Dare and Mr. Samuel Muir will act for me." He turned to the cringing Ruby. "I believe you know of Mr. Muir? He mentioned you to me recently as . . . an *astute* member of his profession." There was no attempt to disguise the scorn the duke felt.

March Wardell, taking his hand down from his reddening cheek, roared with rage. "I'll take you to the highest court in the land for this, you blaggard! Everybody knows what kind of a ——— you are!" He used a very nasty word, which Leslie had never heard before.

Drogo stepped forward and hit him so hard in the jaw that Wardell smashed to the floor.

The other three occupants of the room stared down at

him with varying emotions. Then Drogo said quietly, "Ruby, get that . . . *thing* out of Lady Bella's house. You know my seconds. You had better act as one of his; I doubt he'll find it easy to get another! Arrange the meeting as soon as possible!"

"Surely you jest, Your Grace," shrilled the lawyer. "A *duel*? The constables will prevent it!"

"Only if they are informed that it is to take place," said the duke. "And if they *are* informed, I shall know whom to hold to account, shall I not?" His rigid expression lightened into a taunting smile. "I have fought four duels *à outrance*. And as you see, I am—still here. You might warn your client. He may wish to burnish up his skills with whatever weapon he chooses. It *is* his choice, you know," he explained with insufferable smugness. "As the challenged man."

March Wardell, groaning, was trying to drag himself to his feet.

Drogo regarded him with detached amusement. "Don't try to run out on our duel," he advised, mockingly. "I shall pursue you until we meet on the—*field of honor*. Of course, I use the term loosely." He turned to Ruby. "Get him out of here and advise him as to his safest course of action. It is your responsibility, after all. You permitted him to come here."

The lawyer ignored his staggering client momentarily.

"You are serious about this . . . this duel?"

"Believe it," said the duke, in so cold a voice that Leslie shivered.

Lawyer Ruby led the incoherently muttering Wardell out of the room and out of the house.

In the drawing room, a white-faced Leslie caught at Drogo's arm. "What is a duel *à outrance*?" she asked.

Drogo tried to brush the question aside.

"A very unpleasant fellow, your cousin March," he said loftily. "I am glad you persuaded me to rescue your brother from him."

"What does it mean, Drogo?" Leslie would not let him put her off.

The duke frowned. "It means just what you think it does," he said harshly. "To the death. You are not going to tell me you have tender compassion for that . . . child-murderer."

"I fear for you," said Leslie quietly.

Drogo stared into the deep blue eyes. He had the oddest feeling that if he was not careful, he would drown in their clear, loving depths. He tried for casual amusement.

"I am really a very accomplished swordsman," he began.

"He will cheat," said Leslie grimly. "You will be fired upon from ambush."

"That is why gentlemen have seconds," began Drogo.

"They might bear witness that treachery had occurred," said the girl, "but they could hardly stop the fatal bullet. And you have given that monster the right to choose the weapons."

Staring at her through narrowed lids, Drogo felt a surge of an emotion he had never before experienced. His over-powering impulse was to pick up this darling girl and go with her to some place where they could not be interrupted. And stay there for an undefined period of time. Shaking his head to clear it of this insanity, Drogo said sharply, "You will permit me to deal with this creature in my own way, Leslie. I am scarcely a babe-in-arms!"

The girl said nothing. She kept those disconcerting eyes fastened on his face, and Drogo found himself experiencing a second wave of the strange emotion.

Some positive action was called for.

Drogo took the little female into his arms and held her very tightly. No one had ever really cared whether he lived or died, he thought, in an almost maudlin surge of feeling. *I have got to stop this!* he thought desperately. Decisive action was required!

He bent and took her lips with his, more gently than he had ever possessed a woman's mouth before. Her lips were soft and warm and curiously sweet. Drogo forgot where he was. He even forgot that he had just challenged a cold-blooded murderer to a deadly duel. All he could do was lose himself in the generous tenderness of the girl's kiss.

Then, with a groan, he put the small, enticing body away from him. "You told me you would say *no*!" he gasped.

Leslie's smile was sunlight. "That was to the dangerous men," she said gently.

"*I am dangerous*, you little fool!" Drogo gasped. "Ask anyone!"

"Not to me," said Leslie, with the loving smile that at once enchanted and terrified the noble rake. "Now stop teasing me and let us plan how to protect you from March Wardell."

The Most Noble the Duke of Kenelm stared into the small, concerned, wide-eyed countenance turned up to his. For a moment he felt a sensation of dizziness . . . of *falling*. Catching a deep breath, he seized stern control of his treacherous bodily responses. Assuming a coldly superior expression, he put out both hands to grasp the girl's shoulders and move her a comfortable distance away from him.

The moment he touched the chit, he knew he had made a bad tactical mistake. *Warm . . . soft . . . attractive!* announced his mind, rationally.

Leslie, accepting the clasp of his hands, swayed slightly toward the man, her smile suddenly radiant.

DANGER! shrilled the duke's mind frantically.

Too late.

Drogo Trevelyan was shocked, menaced, overwhelmed by the most terrifying *emotion* he had ever experienced—*Fear*.

With a single, hoarse expletive which neither he nor the girl understood, the Most Noble the Duke of Kenelm turned and ran out of the house.

Chapter 24

After Drogo's abrupt departure, still most unreasonably refusing to permit Leslie to share in his plans for the duel, the girl went immediately to her great-aunt's bedroom and opened the budget.

Lady Bella did not show the surprise Leslie had expected.

"Ring for Cameron," was her first response. "That woman is up to every rig and row in town. And you'd better tell Weems to send up my cocoa," she added, in a falsely fading voice. "I shall need all the sustenance I can get!" She favored Leslie with a bright, admiring glance. " 'Alarums and excursions,' as Shakespeare probably said at least once. I must admit I have not enjoyed myself so much for years! Had I known how very *interesting* it would be to sponsor a clutch of children into the ton, I would have done it ages ago!"

The cocoa having been enjoyed, and Lady Bella and Cameron briefed as to March Wardell's latest move, the conference became a serious war council. Cameron, when pressed for her opinion, said that she was sure the duke could handle so paltry a challenge "with one hand tied behind him."

This image of vulnerability so distressed Leslie that she became quite pale, so that Lady Bella was forced to instruct Cameron to push her head between her knees. When Leslie refused to be so handled, her great-aunt insisted that Cameron pour the child a third cup of cocoa. This was refused.

141

"How can you jest when Drogo's life is at stake?" the girl demanded fiercely.

"Here's heat! Cameron, tell the chit that such lack of control is unacceptable," Lady B instructed.

The dresser surprised them both. Looking somberly at the girl, Cameron said, "I think Lady Leslie has a certain sensitivity to the fate of the duke. Love sometimes bestows that painful gift." While both ladies stared, wide-eyed, Cameron went on, "I do not clearly perceive the future course of events, you understand, but I fail to see any sign of an early death for His Grace. On the contrary . . ."

If Leslie and Lady B had been surprised before, they were now alarmed. The older woman cleared her throat nervously. "Are you claiming to be . . . possessed of . . . ah . . . oracular powers, woman?" she demanded.

Cameron gave her a hard glance. "I make no claims," she said shortly.

Leslie got up impulsively and threw her arms around the dresser's bony shoulders. "I pray that you *are* so possessed," she said, hugging the woman. "Can you promise me that he isn't going to be killed by that monster?"

"There will be no duel," Cameron spoke knowledgeably.

Lady Bella sniffed disparagingly, but, catching the radiance on Leslie's expressive countenance, did not argue the matter. Instead, she cast Cameron a pretty shrewd glance and said, "Well, I called you in here to take advantage of your *nous*. What do you advise us to do?"

"Go back to Endale," said the Scotswoman decisively.

"Go *back*!" Leslie's voice mirrored the horrified revulsion she was feeling. "You cannot mean it!"

"Most unwise," agreed the old bluestocking. "Put the earl back into the power of the Wardells? Insane!"

Cameron's face took on a closed expression. She folded her sinewy hands in front of her, and made no reply to the charge. Fuming, Lady Bella tried to make sense out of the situation. Leslie was white with shock and disappointment. She had truly hoped for a clever plan from the dresser. She squared her shoulders and tried for a smile.

"Thank you, Cameron," she said quietly. "I suppose that, legally speaking, you are correct. I must consult with Lady Bella's advisers today. Perhaps if they cannot be persuaded to fight in the courts for a change of guardians, we will have to go back—"

"Never!" vowed Lady Bella. "I'll . . . I'll take the thing into Chancery, or whatever they call the highest courts. They say a case can go as long as fifty years before those old dodoes get around to giving a decision!"

Light-headed with relief and the joy of the old woman's loyal partisanship, Leslie said merrily, "Given even half that time, Daryl will be well into his majority, and no Wardell will have power to harm him!"

Lady Bella gave the girl an indulgent smile.

"Now go back to your room and let Cameron make you pretty for the day. I'll get up, too. I intend to wait upon my men-of-law this very morning, and set all in train."

With a final, grateful smile, Leslie went quickly out of the room.

Cameron followed silently.

Drogo Trevelyan was also consulting with his lawyer. Muir was delighted with the opportunity to ensnare the recalcitrant nobleman further into county affairs. He began to give his client a brief résumé of the improvements already made on the ducal residence, but Drogo brushed that aside in favor of the more urgent business of securing the safety of the Earl of Endale by placing him under his great-aunt's care.

Muir frowned and pursed his lips. "You say Lady Endale is willing to act as guardian for the children? That might work. She's an odd old creature, but she's accepted as clever and responsible by all of London that matters."

"I wish to help her," said Drogo firmly. "After all, my estate runs with Endale's, and I am a fellow peer." He caught Muir's speculative glance and said hotly, "They are good children, bright and well behaved! *Some one* must protect them from that vile creature!"

"Oh, I quite agree." The lawyer was enjoying his

client's heated response, so dramatically different from the bored arrogance of a few weeks before. "But why must it be . . . *your* protection, Your Grace?"

Refusing to answer the embarrassing question, Drogo blurted out, "I have challenged the fellow to a duel."

Muir's mouth opened and then shut slowly. "A duel? I see." And he scanned the handsome, flushed features with new interest. "Knowing the fellow's propensity for violent action, do you think that a wise decision?"

Drogo shrugged. "Wise or not, it seemed the only course at the time. Wardell had arrived in Lady Bella Endale's town house to carry off the earl. During the course of the . . . discussion, he insulted both Lady Leslie and myself."

"So you called him out," said the lawyer, nodding cheerfully. "Very sensible."

Drogo gave him a resentful glare. "Of course, it wasn't! As I am now well aware. Wardell is vicious, brutal, despicable . . . a commoner!" A reluctant grin touched the duke's lips. "I named you as one of my seconds, Muir. With Kevin O'Dare."

"Alas! There goes my reputation," mourned the lawyer, a smile tugging at his prim lips. "You do know that, as a member of the bar, I cannot serve. I should be compelled by duty to inform the magistrates." His expression of disappointment lightened. "But that's a perfect way of stopping this idiocy!"

"I intend to kill the fellow, and a duel's the only quick, legal way I can think of," protested the duke.

" 'Legal'?" taunted Muir.

"It's been a respected custom here in England for donkey's years," protested Drogo. "And I'm good at it. Four duels and I'm still alive."

"And just where did these barbaric events take place?" demanded the lawyer. Then, "No, on second thought, *don't* inform me. I might have to use it against you at your trial."

"In Europe," grinned Drogo. "Be a sport, Muir! You know you'd enjoy the human *drama* of it all."

"Folly," corrected the old lawyer, firmly repressing a sparkle of amusement. "Who are Wardell's seconds?"

"I told his lawyer, Ruby, that he'd have to act as one of them—"

"Adam Ruby took part in this discussion?" gasped Muir. "There won't be any duel! He's probably informed Bow Street by this time! It's the perfect way to save his client," he added, approvingly.

"I hope he has," Drogo surprised his lawyer by saying. "With what I've already told them about Wardell, this will form one more piece of provocative evidence."

Muir looked at his difficult client with a mixture of exasperation and reluctant admiration. "Against whom?" he murmured, and then, with a firm authority seldom evident in his dealings with this arrogant nobleman, he said, "You will be guided by me in this, Kenelm, if you please! Whatever your original intent, you have handled the matter excellently. There will be no duel. I shall have a clerk inform Bow Street anonymously, in case Ruby has neglected to do so. Oh, do not be alarmed."—catching the look of frustrated anger on his client's face—"Justice will be served, I promise you. I'll meet again with Lady Bella's lawyers and propose a joint guardianship. I think we can outwit Adam Ruby!" He permitted himself a genteel sneer. Then he continued thoughtfully, "I agree that the man Wardell is dangerous—mostly because he is too stupid to foresee the effects of his own activities. He would never get away with killing the child whose heir he is," Muir added.

For some reason this would-be soothing comment enraged the duke. "Oh, splendid!" he snapped. "Wardell will land himself in gaol—*after he has killed little Daryl!*"

Driving away from Muir's chambers with the echo of the lawyer's gentle laughter in his ears, Drogo realized that he would have to get himself in hand. Why was he, a hardened, cynical worldling of twenty-nine thoroughly lived years, running like a frightened boy from a seventeen-year-old chit with big blue eyes? Drogo knew that if he discussed the matter with Kevin, that Irish rake would suggest a little romp with Venus as a cure-all. But Drogo definitely did not desire such a nostrum. The little witch had ensnared him; let her be the one to work the cure! Oddly heartened by this decision, Drogo decided to look the chit up the very next day—if not sooner!

And in Cavendish Square, a dowdy black coach drove slowly along in front of Endale Town house. At the exit from the square, it was summarily stopped and the door flung open by a Bow Street runner. The coach proved to be empty. The coachman insisted that he had been hired by some totty-head to drive round the square and then go back to his stand.

Shrugging, the runner let him go.

There was no use trying to understand the quirks of the quality. And after all, there'd been no harm done.

Chapter 25

A missive was delivered in Cavendish Square while Lady Bella and Leslie were in town conducting a most satisfactory session with the Endale family lawyers. The senior partner, who had never really *taken* to March Wardell, informed them that he had had a note from Kenelm's lawyer, Samuel Muir, offering all possible support for Lady Bella's plan to assume guardianship of the young Endales. Mr. Foley even expressed confidence that the changeover would not take too long nor be too difficult of achievement.

Arriving home flushed with triumph, the ladies discovered the message from the Countess de Lieven, which contained an invitation from the patronesses of Almack's for Lady Bella and her niece, Lady Leslie, to attend a small function on Friday evening.

Lady Bella's delight was obvious. "We've done it, child! Almack's! The supreme accolade! Whatever shall we wear?"

Choking down a giggle, Leslie mentioned several of the more striking of Lady Bella's gowns. All were rejected with every sign of loathing. "No, child, we must go to Eugenie and enlist her aid. Unless you think that Kenelm might be prevailed upon to advise us." She finished with a speculative glance at Leslie.

The idea was tempting, Leslie admitted. Still, a refusal would be very painful. She frowned, her blue eyes reflecting deep thought. At length she turned to Lady B and smiled.

"I'll ask him, ma'am. But you know what he is! He is as likely to send us to Coventry as to help us."

The old woman nodded cheerfully. "We'll take our chances, dear child. Kenelm's already put himself out for young Daryl, from what Foley said today." Momentarily caught by another idea, she sniffed. "Foley! The man should be called *Fogey*, don't you agree? Pompous old natterer!"

No longer controlling her desire to laugh, Leslie said teasingly, "Aunt Bella, you had that poor man bewitched! I was expecting him to offer you a partnership."

Lady Bella preened a little. "I did have some rather sensible questions to ask, and pertinent suggestions to make, did I not?" she agreed. "Do you think Mr. Foley is . . . good looking?"

"We shall be able to tell when he brings the documents for your signature tomorrow, shall we not?" Leslie replied demurely. "I thought you said these lawyers dawdled on for an age. Mr. Foley seems to waste very little time! You seem to have had a powerful influence upon the . . . er . . . pompous old natterer."

"Naughty child," reproved Lady Bella, but she was plainly pleased at the gentle impeachment.

In the event, Drogo Trevelyan appeared to be quite willing to assist the Endale ladies to acquire garments suitable for a first appearance at Almack's. Lady Bella was delighted with the French Empire style Eugenie selected for her. The velvet draped her aged bones softly, and the dark rose color lent her a charming blush. The rose velvet turban was effectively draped to disguise her gray hair.

"When Cameron gets through with me, I shall, to use Daryl's words, look as fine as fivepence!" she said with satisfaction. "Now, what magic have you for my great-niece, Madame Eugenie?"

The duke interrupted with a roguish smile. He seemed, decided Leslie happily, to have gotten over whatever mood it was that had sent him scuttling from Lady Bella's home

148

with such an uncharacteristic loss of poise. He was standing at Leslie's shoulder, smiling down into her eyes.

"Have you a pretty dress in a color to match these lovely eyes?" he asked softly.

Leslie decided that life could hold no more enchanting moment.

Chapter 26

While Lawyer Muir was contentedly weaving his web, and Drogo was attempting to drown his incomprehensible new emotions with the surprised but willing cooperation of his friend Kevin, another sort of conference was taking place in a small, unobtrusive hostel in an unfashionable section of London. There, in the suite they had shared under an assumed name ever since Wardell's agent had located the runaway earl, a one-sided discussion was going on between March and his stolid, low-voiced wife Charity.

March was seated at a table, steadily lowering the level of the whiskey in a bottle he had ordered with dinner. Predictably, the liquor was serving only to exacerbate the horror he felt at the situation that damned nobleman had trapped him into.

"*A duel, for God's sake!*" he muttered with a curse. The things were outlawed! He had only to inform on Kenelm, he told his wife belligerently, and the damned lecherous bully would be in gaol where he belonged!

Charity Moggs Wardell had been listening to her husband for half an hour, her small button-black eyes intent under puffy lids. At the conclusion of his latest outburst, she spoke in that low, gravelly voice that always intimidated her husband.

"You have botched the matter from the outset, Mr. Wardell," she said grimly. "I shall put my own plan into action now."

Wardell stared at her with red-rimmed eyes. He knew

better than to try to argue with the only child and heiress of Gamaliel Moggs, who had been smart enough to rig the marriage settlements so that his daughter and only child held control of his enormous fortune—and to provide that, upon her death, the residue of the estate should be given to the Crown. It seemed he had correctly gauged the quality of Charity's suitor.

Mrs. Wardell was not waiting for her husband's approval of her plan. "You had better go back to our town house in the morning," she told him. "Stay there, where the servants, and any spies of Kenelm's, can attest to your presence. That will clear you of suspicion when I act. Tell everyone we have been on a trip, and that I am visiting friends for a few more days. Above all, *do nothing against the earl*. I shall handle the problem myself." She shot a keen, curiously unfeminine glance at the man she had accepted as her husband solely because he was the heir to an earldom. Then, without further ado, Mrs. Wardell left the room.

The following morning Lady B and Leslie were closeted with Cameron, preparing for the reception that evening at Almack's. Cameron was silent, but since that was her usual style, the two ladies did not think to comment. Instead they consulted the dresser as to the merits of the costumes they had chosen for an event neither had ever attended before.

"You do well to wear the rose velvet, milady," Cameron advised. "With the matching turban and your diamond parure, it should prove both correct for such a social event, and flattering to your hostesses." She turned to the eagerly waiting girl. "I have sorted through your new gowns carefully, Lady Leslie. This new one chosen by His Grace is the right one."

The dresser took from an armoire a silken robe of a blue that exactly matched Leslie's eyes. Drogo had smiled when he chose it, she recalled, and made some laughing comment to Eugenie, who was completely under the rascal's spell. The woman had even found a pair of blue silk-covered shoes that matched the gown.

151

Viewing the soft, delicate garment now, Leslie sighed with pleasure. "It is the prettiest dress I have ever had."

"I suppose you are going to tell me I must not give my niece any jewelry, Cameron," fussed the old woman. "Just trumpery roses?"

"No, milady, I am going to suggest that you give her the pearl choker with the sapphire at the front."

"My grandmother's pearls," agreed Lady B happily. "Most becoming—and suitable, you think?" They exchanged glances.

"But they are priceless!" protested Leslie. Everyone in the beau monde knew about Countess Amanda's necklace! A symbol of true love purchased by her young husband after a search throughout most of Europe for "a bauble to adorn the prettiest throat in all England," the young husband had ardently proclaimed. "They are too . . . important to be wasted on a plain little female like myself!"

Both Cameron and Lady Bella ignored her half-hearted protests. In fact, Cameron told her quite severely to stop havering and sit down at once so her hair could be washed, since it would require the whole day for the dresser to prepare *two* ladies for the coming evening's activities.

Shortly before the duke was expected to arrive to escort the two Endale ladies to Almack's, they came down the staircase *en grande tenue*, to the vociferous admiration of the three younger Endales, who had been permitted to stay up long enough to behold the dazzling parade.

"You are positively magnificent, Aunt Bella!" cried Hilary, clasping her hands with admiration.

The old woman made a stately curtsy, to the children's delight. Daryl came forward to bow over her hand, and Meredith kissed the delicately painted cheek.

And then the children's eyes went to their sister, coming down the stairs far enough behind Lady Bella so as not to steal her thunder. And this time the young Endales were silent, until Daryl came forward and offered his hand to lead Leslie down the last few steps, and Hilary gasped.

"Is it really *you*, Leslie? But you are beautiful!"

Indeed, in the golden light of the many candles, the girl had a glowing aura of tender young loveliness.

Meredith said it for all of them. "I doubt very much if Drogo Trevelyan will be able to resist you tonight, Leslie."

Two footmen were at the doors, swinging them open. There was the sound of a heavy vehicle drawing up, and Weems was making ready to assist the ladies down the steps and into the duke's carriage himself, when a neatly dressed groom swung down off the box and ran lightly up the steps.

"Urgent message for Lady Leslie Endale," he gasped. "From His Grace! Begs to inform you he is most unfortunately compelled to excuse himself, and dares not hope you might be willing to wait for him. Respectfully urges you go ahead without him!" gasped the groom, with the air of one successfully completing a long and well-rehearsed announcement.

The Endales, all five of them, stared at one another in shocked surprise.

"I would have sworn Kenelm would never do such a thing," Lady Bella said dully. "Of course we cannot go without him."

Hilary, already in tears, agreed. "So humiliating! Everyone would think he has begged off because he doesn't like us!"

"But he *does* like us!" argued Daryl. "I know he does! He *talks to me*!"

Leslie, who had clutched the newel post, turned a pallid face to her distressed family. "Of course he likes us," she said grimly. "It's *the duel*!"

There was an appalled silence, and then Lady Bella said sharply, "Nonsense! No person in his senses would fight a duel at night! He couldn't see to aim the pistol."

This remark did little to comfort any of those who heard it. Meredith spoke up bravely, "It may have been some totty-headed notion of March Wardell's. As the one challenged, he can determine the details. But Drogo Trevelyan

153

is too downy a bird to be taken in by tricks, Leslie. You know that! He'll make sure it's a fair fight."

"And if he doesn't, his friend Kevin O'Dare will be there—a great gun, Leslie, I assure you!" said Daryl confidently. The others hastened to agree.

Leslie, hungry for their assurances, noticed that the groom who had delivered the message still lingered just within the doorway. *As though he has a private message to impart*, thought the girl, grasping at any hope. She moved toward him, and said in an urgent whisper, "Was there a word for me, groom? I am Lady Leslie."

The young fellow's expression brightened. "Yus, ma'am! I was told to tell you, if I got a chance to speak privatelike, that the . . . the dool is to take place on the heath where th' balloon went up. Said you'd know where that was."

"What is the fellow saying to you?" demanded Lady Bella, sweeping down on the whispering pair like a man-of-war under full sail.

Casting a fearful glance at the formidable dame, the groom whispered, "I'm to wait for ye, Miss," and nipped off down the steps to mount the box. The carriage lumbered away.

"What did the boy say?" repeated the old woman.

Leslie was in a quandary. If she told her great-aunt what the groom had said, Lady Bella would of course refuse to let her go to the heath, which Leslie had every intention of doing. Drogo would not have told her where the meeting was to take place if he had wished her to stay away. It gave the girl a warm glow in her breast to think that the duke wished her to support him in this vital moment. Perhaps she might bring him luck.

Leslie knew very little about duels. She had, of course, never seen one, nor had the subject been introduced into any family conversation she could recall. Still, Miss Wheaton had made a few casual references to the art of dueling as it related to chivalry, so Leslie was aware that ladies often gave a token for good luck to a knight who fought to defend their honor. She made up her mind.

"He was telling me that actually, His Grace would rather we went quietly to bed. He assures me he will explain everything to Lady Jersey and the Countess de Lieven. No doubt we shall be invited to Almack's upon another occasion," she finished airily.

Lady Bella regarded her with suspicion and deep disappointment. Finally, with great annoyance, she uttered the single syllable, *"Men!"* and stamped back upstairs to her bedroom.

Hilary concurred with the sentiment. "He should never have permitted the duel to be set on the night you were attending Almack's for the first time," she said with disgust. "It shows a lack of . . . of sensibility!"

Daryl chuckled, and opened his mouth to make a masculine comment upon the relative importance of duels and receptions, but catching sight of Leslie's pale face, he forbore. Meredith gently shepherded her siblings up to their rooms, only pausing to bestow a comforting kiss on Leslie's pale cheek. Leslie waited just inside the drawing room until everyone, even Weems, had sadly disappeared. Then she caught up her cloak and slipped silently out the front door.

As she expected, the duke's massive carriage was waiting just down the street from Lady Bella's house. The door was hanging open. At her hurried approach, the groom swung down and boosted her into the darkened interior with more haste than grace. Then, with a rumble of heavy wheels, the carriage jolted off through the darkened streets.

Oh, Drogo—be safe! prayed the girl.

Five minutes later, the great coach of the Duke of Kenelm was pulled up before Endale Town house, and Drogo, magnificent in dark blue velvet to complement his little charmer, ran lightly up the front steps and banged happily upon the knocker. As his summons was slow to bring a response, a frown settled over the arrogant, handsome features. *Where was everyone?* Usually a butler as adept as Weems would have had the doors open and the ladies waiting in the hallway!

When one door finally swung open, the Duke of Kenelm was at his most arrogant. Only the sight of the shock and dismay on Weems's countenance gave him pause.

"Your Grace! We just had your message . . . ! *Oh, no!*" And without another word of explanation, Weems turned and ran up the great stairway to fetch Lady Bella.

It took several minutes to share the damaging information, and five more to ascertain that Lady Leslie was no longer in the house.

"March Wardell!" gritted the duke. "I shall kill him!"

Chapter 27

"But why *Leslie*?" groaned Lady Bella. "I thought it was young Daryl he was anxious to kill!"

At this second use of the dreadful word in as many minutes, Hilary, hanging over the upper balcony in desperate anxiety to hear what was going on, emitted such a piercing wail as to bring the adults in the hallway below her back to their senses.

Mastering his panic, Drogo forced a smile. "I'll go after them at once." He attempted to soothe the frightened women. "I believe Wardell will not attempt the drive to Endale. Too easy for a rider on a fast horse to catch up with him! The fellow has a house here in London, does he not? I shall try there first."

"Get O'Dare and a brace of pistols," advised the little earl. "Oh, I wish I might come with you!"

Drogo spared him a comradely grin. "You will be needed here to support Lady Bella and your sisters," he told the boy.

"I never get to share the adventures," protested Daryl.

"Don't be absurd," Hilary chided him. "We all shared a hideous adventure, escaping from Wardell through the woods. And now we see it was all to no avail!" she wept.

"How can you be sure he will take Leslie to his London house?" asked Meredith quietly. "I would think he'd know that's the first place you would search."

Drogo stared into the small pale face. *Hell and damna-*

157

tion! The child was right! Drogo ground his teeth in frustrated fury. *Where would the dastard take Leslie?*

"Send for Mr. O'Dare and the pistols," said Lady Bella heavily. "I'll have Weems notify Mr. Foley and the authorities at Bow Street—"

"Yes, you must do that," agreed Drogo, forcing himself to be calm. "I think I will speak to the runner who is guarding the square, and ask him what he knows about this business."

Lady Bella had enough *nous* to realize that the nobleman would refuse to dawdle about being questioned by officials while Leslie was in such great danger. She also knew that it would be equally useless to try to send the children to bed while matters were in this state. Nodding to the hovering Weems, she requested brandy for the duke and hot cocoa for everyone else.

Drogo gave her his charming smile. "I shall take you up on that when I bring Leslie back to you, ma'am," he said gently. The thought crossed his mind, as he smiled reassuringly at the ring of anxious, loving faces turned so trustingly to his, that, willy-nilly, he had apparently acquired *a family* in the last few weeks. He decided he rather liked the feeling.

And then, with an encouraging wave, he was out the door and standing on the front porch. "Bow Street!" he bellowed. "The runner—*front and center*!"

Out of the trees in the park across the street strode a tall figure with a reassuringly militant bearing. The runner, obviously an old soldier, saluted and gave his name and rank. "'Orace Bardy, sir. Constable."

"I am the Duke of Kenelm," said Drogo. "Your chief has provided Lady Endale with your protection at my request. Tonight, someone persuaded Lady Leslie to go with him in a carriage. Did you witness the departure?"

Why am I babbling on like a pompous idiot when darling little Leslie may be—Drogo could not bear to finish the thought. Only the knowledge that he really had no idea where to look for the girl kept him standing here like a dolt. But it began to appear that the precautions he had taken earlier had had some value after all, for Bardy said carefully, "I saw this big carriage pull up. It was an 'and-some one, milord, and since I'd been warned yer lordship was comin' to pick up the ledies tonight, I wasn't alarmed. A grum jumps out and runs up to the door. I was wonderin' why the nob didn' get out to escort his ledy 'imself." Since Drogo made no answer to this irrelevance, Bardy went on, "After a few minutes the grum comes runnin' down, gets back on the box, an' the coachman drives down the road a piece. When 'e stops, and the grum opens the door, I gets leery. Then, jus' when I'm thinkin' I ought to go over and find out wot's to do, a young ledy slips out of the Endale 'ouse and runs to the carriage. Grum boosts 'er in and slams the door and they're off an' runnin.'"

"I wish you had gone off after them," groaned the duke. "We believe that March Wardell ran some rig on Lady Leslie, to get her to go with him in the coach."

"That's all right, sir," said Constable Bardy. "Yer own grum was watchin' from the park, already mounted an' ready to follow your carriage in case of accidentslike. When 'e saw the little ledy gettin' into a strange coach, 'e jus' . . . followed."

Drogo's relief was so great that for a moment he felt dizzy. "Will he report back here, do you think, Bardy?"

The runner pondered. "I sh'd think 'e would report to your own 'ouse, sir. 'Eadquarterslike."

"Thank you, Bardy! I'll see you get credit for a fine job of surveillance. Report to Bow Street everything which has occurred, and what measures we are taking." Drogo strode back to his own carriage, sent a groom to relate the news to the Endales, and then gave his coachman the order to spring them back to Kenelm Town house. While he awaited the report he knew would be coming as rapidly as was humanly possible, he could alert Muir and Kevin—and collect his pistols.

His carriage was just drawing up in front of his own imposing mansion when a chilling thought struck. *Fool that he was, he had left the earl to all intents and purposes unguarded!* Bardy had been dispatched to report to Bow

Street; his own groom was trailing Leslie in the mysterious carriage. The defenders had been lured away. Endale was unprotected!

Desperately he tried to convince himself that his fears were groundless, that he was attributing greater deviousness to Wardell than the man possessed. Still, the dreadful apprehension would not disappear—in fact, it grew stronger. When his carriage drew up in front of his town residence, Drogo did not wait for the groom to open the door. He flung himself out and up to the massive portal, beating a heavy tattoo until his affronted butler Adam flung them open.

"Send a groom for Mr. O'Dare," Drogo commanded. "Tell him the little Endale is threatened with kidnapping or worse. He is to go to Lady Bella Endale's home in Cavendish Square at once, and *keep his eye on the boy!*"

While he was giving his orders, Drogo had been moving rapidly. He had gone to his library and removed the case containing his dueling pistols. Tucking a handful of bullets into one pocket of his elegant velvet coat, he had returned to the entrance hall.

"Tell the stableboy to saddle up Ajax—on the double!" he told Adam. "Then get me a sensible riding cloak! I look like a Bond Street cavalier on the strut!"

He was forced to grin at the indignant expression on the old servant's face, but there was no time for apologies. In fact, he decided, he would save time if he went out to the stable in the mews and set off as soon as Ajax was ready.

Again he caught himself up. *Set off to where?* The young groom, whose name he did not even know, had not yet reported! It might be *tomorrow* before he had news . . . and Leslie might be—*No!* Sweat broke out on the wide brow as Drogo fought his battle for control of the devastating fears that racked him.

Just after midnight, the first news came. It was heralded by the loud clatter of hooves and some masculine shouts. Drogo was at the open front door almost as soon as the butler. Kevin O'Dare ran up the steps, laughing.

160

"We caught him, Drogo! We have the skelpin! He won't be trying to pull off any more chancy tricks for a while, I'll wager!"

"The child!" demanded Drogo. "Is Daryl safe?"

"The little earl is safe, I tell you!" Kevin's elated voice rang out. "We were hiding when Wardell came, demanding to talk to Lady Bella. Thought he'd have only an old woman and some servants to deal with, you see! Two of the runners, me, and my cousin were behind one of those Oriental screens, listening to the whole thing! Wardell offered to exchange the young earl—his legal ward, he boasted, and rightfully under his control—for Lady Leslie. Just as he was beginning to threaten the poor old woman, the screen fell over with a crash and we had to end the farce!" He grinned ruefully. "The runners are a stiff-rumped crew," he murmured. "They only let me hit the blaggard twice before they marched him away to Bow Street."

While the duke said and did all that was hospitable and admiring, he was quite unable to disguise the deep alarm he felt over the missing girl. And finally Kevin sensed the tension in his friend, and offered to come with him as soon as they had news of her whereabouts. To this generous offer the duke gave thanks, but told his friend to go home and get some rest, since he would have to attend the arraignment of Wardell the following morning, and would need all his wits about him.

"Muir will help you to see that he does not escape his due punishment," Drogo told his friend, "but you must be there to testify."

In the event, it was a short time later when Derry, the young groom, pounded up the street, jumped off his horse, left it blowing and frothy in front of the mansion, and raced up the steps and in the door, which had been left ajar. Hearing the noise of his arrival, Drogo strode out into the hallway to question him.

"They've got Miss pent up in a grubby little inn about an 'alf hour's 'ard ride north o' Lunnon," the youth gasped. "I seen 'em un'itch the 'orses, so I figures they're set for the night!" He proceeded to give the duke careful directions for reaching the place.

"Well done, boy," said his master. Then, "What is your name? I can't keep calling you boy when you've done a *man's job*."

"I'm Derry, Your Grace," grinned the groom.

"Give Derry anything he asks for," commanded Drogo, turning to run back to the stables. "I'll thank you personally later, Derry," he promised.

Beaming with triumph, the lad began to think of what all he might ask for under the duke's lavish edict.

It was not hard for Drogo to follow Derry's directions. When he was several hundred yards from the squalid little inn, he led a weary Ajax onto the grassy verge beside the road, to muffle the sound of their approach. There was a light burning in one room on the second floor. All else was dark—and silent. Grasping one of his pistols, which he had charged during the hideous wait for news, Drogo dismounted and tied Ajax to a shrub near the road. Then he approached the building and tried the front door.

Surprisingly, it opened easily.

Drogo crept cautiously up the sagging wooden steps to the second floor. Oddly enough, he was reminded of his first furtive advance upon the Endale children, when he had thought them gypsy thieves.

The upper hall was narrow and malodorous. There was a thin streak of light around an ill-fitting door halfway down the short hall. Drogo moved stealthily toward it. Grasping the pistol firmly, he drew back his foot and kicked in the door.

His intent gaze swept the wretched room, taking in the dusty, rumpled bed, the tattered drapes, the broken window. . . . And then he saw her. Leslie was huddled in the corner next to the window, a shard of the heavy glass in one hand, glaring defiantly at—Charity Wardell!

Moving slowly out of the shadows, the heavyset woman, clothed in her usual sober black, her sandy hair hanging in

162

loose strands around her face and neck, advanced toward the man who had just effected a rude entry to the room. Her small mouth was a rictus of hate, fear, rage. Drogo was afraid that, in her frenzy of disappointment, she might try to do Leslie an injury. She did not appear to have a weapon. The big man relaxed his vigilance slightly as he glanced again at the slender, defiant girl.

Leslie! So great a joy to find you safe!

Drogo drew a deep breath. "I believe it is time you left for London, ma'am," he told Mrs. Wardell gently. "Your husband needs you. He has been arrested for attempted kidnapping and is at present being held in the cells at Bow Street."

Slowly the raddled face turned aside from its rigid perusal of the big man standing just inside the doorway. Charity Wardell faced the girl. Leslie had lowered her arm. Now she dropped her makeshift weapon. The glass crashed and shattered on the wooden floor as Leslie took a step, two steps, toward Drogo. Her expression began to soften and glow with adoration for her rescuer.

And then Charity Wardell struck.

A tiny gleam of light was all the warning Drogo got, as the half-crazed woman lashed out at Leslie with a small knife. Instantly chaos reigned in the grubby little room. The woman was raving now, cursing her husband in a guttural flow, and striking about her in a fury. Drogo could have waited his chance to seize her, but he was too fearful that she might injure the girl—who was evidently suffering from the same fears for his person.

It was a nightmare scene. The fitful gusts of wind coming through the broken pane twisted the flame of the candle, making shifting shadows which added to the menacing power of the crazed woman's knife. If he had been willing to hurt her, Drogo could have rendered her harmless with a single blow. Instead, in an agony of fear for his intrepid little shieldmate, he maneuvered Mrs. Wardell into a corner and, catching her sinewy wrists in one hand, he seized the knife with the other.

When she realized she had been disarmed, the woman staggered over to the bed and collapsed on it, weeping.

Drogo led Leslie out into the dirty hall.

"Did she hurt you?"

Leslie raised her lovely eyes to his face. They were shadowed with weariness and remembered fear, but they glowed with an emotion that alarmed the duke.

"No, Drogo, she didn't hurt me. She was planning to send a message to you—to make an exchange."

Drogo shook his head as he led her toward the rickety stairway. "She is mad! What did they hope to accomplish by this ploy? The husband already tried to make off with Daryl—and failed," he added quickly.

"She told me she planned to bargain. To trade me in exchange for control of Daryl. She thought they could force you to accept Wardell as his guardian. She said you had a . . . weakness for me." She could not meet his gaze. "Perhaps the *on dits* misled her?"

Drogo felt again the onset of that weird vertigo that had so disturbed him in other encounters with this girl. He had fully intended to be calm, kindly, and controlled when he found the chit, but she was having her usual effect upon his nerves, and he resented it. He opened his lips to make a laughing comment concerning the absurdity of the rumors circulating in the ton, and instead, he heard himself saying, in a voice he did not recognize as his own, "You looked so small and dear and fierce in that squalid room! So brave and beautiful! Your eyes were blazing sapphires—the exact color of your dress. . . ." His golden gaze caressed her face.

Through the girl's mind flashed Cameron's dream: the stairway, the blue dress, and true love at the foot of the stairs! She gave her true love a weary, adoring smile.

"You came," she said softly. "Mrs. Wardell had promised to kill me if you refused to bargain with her. But you outwitted her! You found me. You saved me. I love you."

This far-too-forthright statement sent a chill of terror through the nobleman's well-armored heart. He had learned, in the hardest of schools, that vulnerability meant

164

pain—either the mockery of his peers or, even more devastating, the inevitable betrayal and loss. He struck out blindly.

"But I do not love you, child. How could I? You are scarcely out of the nursery, so green a girl that you would bore me after three days." Avoiding the pain in the vulnerable little face—*it was for her own good, wasn't it?—better a little pain now than a great deal later,* he knew that—Drogo dealt the final blow.

"If ever I do marry, it will only be to secure the succession. And you are not old enough to be a suitable mother to my children."

Drogo waited, avoiding her glance. Would she argue, plead?

After a long moment, Leslie said in a voice from which all feeling had been removed, "I see. Then shall we return to Lady Bella at once?"

Oddly annoyed at her instant acceptance of his crushing rebuff, the duke grasped Leslie's arm and pulled her down the stairs. The sooner he got her—and himself—out of this abominable situation, the better he would like it! She was no different from any of the vapid young debutantes he had been forced to meet over the years, he told himself grimly. One minute they were passionately in love with one man; the next, they could hardly remember his name as they swooned over some other unfortunate male! Somehow, he had not thought of Leslie as that sort of girl! It goes to show, Drogo decided cynically, that one female is very much like another—and all of them are deceitful.

Yet he would have wagered his life that Leslie Endale was different!

Chapter 28

To his surprise, Drogo discovered that he was shaking with anger as he pulled the little female up in front of him on Ajax and anchored her firmly against his chest. The fact that it was very *satisfying* to hold her so roughly did not for a moment diminish his sense of outrage—*Outrage?* Well, of course he was furious at her stupidity in swallowing whole the absurd trick of Mrs. Wardell. Like a trout with a lure, he thought in disgust. He surely was not angry at her instant acceptance of his rebuff! He clenched her softness unnecessarily close to his body as a method of informing her that he could hardly wait to get her back to her family and be free of the responsibility!

He gave Ajax the office to walk. A slow pace would make the return tediously long, but the simplest concern for the noble animal, forced to bear a double burden, and having already performed splendidly in the punishing ride from London, demanded such consideration. No doubt the beast was tired by their frantic pursuit of the maddening girl in his arms. Leslie chose this unfortunate moment to ask a question.

"Where is your carriage?" she faltered. She was confused by Drogo's obvious anger, after his heroic rescue and especially after the magical moment they had shared—and his cruel rebuff immediately after. Had her response been too timid? Too enthusiastic? She had accepted his rejection. Why was he so angry with her?

Her noble duke lost no time in enlightening her.

"My carriage, is it?" he began with awful intensity. "Of course I left it in London, in front of Lady Endale's town house, where I had brought it to take you and your Aunt to Almack's! Or had you forgotten my invitation?"

Leslie decided she had better cut at once to the heart of the matter. It seemed Drogo was angry at her for her folly in being so easily gulled by the Wardells!

"Your—that is, the Wardells' groom told us you could not attend the reception with us. That you were to fight a duel on the heath where the balloon ascent took place . . . and that you wanted me with you . . ." Her voice weakened and died against the furious incredulity that was somehow radiating from his big hard body to her own.

Drogo did not spare her. "You actually *believed* that I would permit anything to change my plans after my invitation had been accepted?" he began harshly. "It is clear you do not know me! You believed I would arrange a *duel*, at *midnight*, on the *heath*?" For a moment, the duke's innate sense of fair play overcame his rage, and he admitted grudgingly, "The heath might have been a suitable venue, considering that Wardell could hardly conceal any assassins in such open country." However, this softening of his anger did not last, and with an unconscious tightening of his already tight clasp of her person, Drogo continued his tirade.

"So, having totty-headedly accepted all these ridiculous assumptions about me and my code of behavior, you sneaked clandestinely from your aunt's home, entered a strange carriage at night, and blithely set out for an unknown destination?"

Leslie was feeling crushed in more ways than one. And cold, and too warm where she was in contact with His Grace, and lonelier than she had ever felt in her life. That may have been the reason for her anguished wail, "But I *did* know my destination! I was going to the heath where we watched the balloon ascent and were . . . so *happy*! I was going to be your . . . your second in the duel—"

Even as she spoke these words, her mind told her how absurd they must sound. Her mind was right.

"Indeed?" said the duke coldly. "My second, is it? Do you have absolutely no conception of the way the Polite World goes on? There has never—*never*—to my knowledge been an occasion upon which a *female* has acted as a second in a duel. Certainly not in England," he tacked on pompously.

Then, as if this tongue-lashing were not enough, the duke went on coldly, "Not content with accepting this bizarre proposal from an unvouched-for servant, you proceeded to slip away without informing your elderly relative or your siblings of your intent, thus causing them extreme alarm and concern. Poor little Hilary," he finished accusingly, "was in tears."

Something within Leslie put its foot down. *Enough!* Enough of this arrogance, this harsh cruelty to a battered heroine. Did he think this evening had been like a charming soiree in an elegant drawing room for *her*? Defiantly Leslie flung her head back, only to collide painfully with an iron-clad chest. This injury, added to the insult of the duke's scornful charges, served to unleash the girl's own fury.

"Hilary," she riposted scornfully if inaccurately, "is *always* in tears. When she is not in alt over the . . . the condescending courtesies of her *Benefactor*! I should think that even the little exposure you have had to us awkward and ignorant Endales would have told you that—with *your famous nous*!"

A new kind of excitement began to burn in the duke's breast. *Fight back at him, would she?* He'd see that! Settling the maddening little armful more cozily against his torso, where it was already beginning to generate a delightful warmth, he said in a voice he tried to make scornful, "Oh, I shall probably have my work cut out for me, whipping you Endales into shape! I am to be your new guardian, you know—along with Lady Bella."

Leslie digested this earthshaking news. Her guardian? Did that mean he would not be able to pursue a . . . closer relationship? Did he *wish* to pursue a closer relationship, or had his behavior in that terrible room been some aberration of the senses—his and hers? She wished she knew! Dared she ask? Leslie sank limply against the duke's iron warmth, confessing that she really had no notion how one might handle so overpowering a nobleman.

At that moment the inspiration came to her like a veritable bolt of lightning. From a thoroughly English, unimpeachable source!

"Does being our guardian mean that you will have to arrange suitable marriages for all of us?" she began.

This startling inquiry so shocked His Grace that he felt a cold chill, or *grue* as the Scots have it, run over his whole body. Gathering his forces hastily, he tried for a smooth recover. The gazetted rake bent an accusing glare at the small female who had asked such an outrageously indiscreet question.

"Why do you ask? Have you someone in mind for yourself?" he demanded. Just as he thought: Off with the old; on with the new!

"Yes," said the incorrigible little female.

"May a mere guardian be permitted to ask the name of this fortunate man?" Drogo asked with awful courtesy.

"Why, it is yourself, of course," said Leslie outrageously, tilting her face up to offer him her lovely smile. "No lesser man will satisfy me. After what you said, and I said, and you did, up in that hallway— You said," she reminded him, "that I was small and dear and brave and beautiful. And fierce," she added warningly. "You were right. I shall fight to have you, dearest Drogo."

"Stop!" gasped the embattled duke. "What *I* said . . ." he found the memory of the moment she had conjured up so arousing that he had not the heart to deny the thrill of pleasure her announcement of her claim gave him. She really wanted him . . . *loved* him? "You intend to fight for me?" he asked.

"A *worthy* guardian would be asking what the *man's* intentions were," the chit informed him pertly.

Drogo's mind joined his senses in a reeling dance. Was his Leslie teasing him? Did she dare to try to run a rig on the downiest, wariest, wisest bird of prey in England?

Glaring down into her shining eyes, he decided that, indeed, she would dare to fight for what she truly desired. He pulled her closer to his heated body, eliminating the tiny space his shocked response to her challenge had created.

"So you wish to marry me, do you?"

"Oh, *yes*, Drogo," said his little love, like a vow, like a prayer.

Drogo drew in a shaking breath of sheer delight.

"Hooked at last," he muttered, grinning widely down into the enchanting, adorable, teasing little face. "Well, I suppose I must arrange it. Since I already seem to have acquired a family, including one literary great-aunt, one underage nobleman, and two diverse but darling sisters, I suppose there is nothing left for me to do but give them a mother!" Noting the look of bliss on her countenance, he went on in an unsteady voice, "And myself the dearest, bravest, most maddening little wife any guardian ever chose for himself! Kiss me, Wife!"

Before the utter bliss of Drogo's warm lips quite overcame her senses, Leslie remembered to say, "Don't forget I am to be the mother to all your own sons and daughters, when we have them!"

Dazed by his unbelievable good fortune, the chosen man pulled her closer to his body. Through his mind flashed a picture of Kenelm Place, restored to its former splendor, dreaming in warm sunlight, its gracious halls ringing with the sounds of children's laughter—beloved children, confident of their parents' love. "I am so glad you found me, little one," he whispered, sealing her lips to his in a tender kiss.

Leslie congratulated herself upon remembering Lady Bella's excellent advice. She would never have found the courage to claim her wonderful Drogo if she had not had the support of her literary great-aunt and an even greater authority.

Had not the elderly bluestocking stated, when the duke had brought them home after the Pentacles' Ball:

> If it were done when 'tis done, then 'twere well
> It were done quickly.

Leslie sighed with rapture and wriggled a little closer into her man's hard embrace. Shakespeare was never wrong!